A SIGN FOR MURDER

A gripping murder mystery full of twists

LINDA MATHER

The Zodiac Mysteries Book 2

Originally published as
Beware Taurus

JOFFE BOOKS

Revised edition 2021
Joffe Books, London
www.joffebooks.com

First published by Macmillan in Great Britain in 1994
as *Beware Taurus*

Cover art by Dee Dee Book Covers

ISBN: 978-1-78931-829-6

To Wendy

PREDICTIONS FOR THE WEEK
BEGINNING 14 JUNE:

TAURUS (22 April—21 May)

You may find yourself on the horns of a dilemma this week — even facing some danger, so beware! Take a step back and try not to be too absorbed in your own plans. A friend or colleague might just be leading you by the ring in your nose so watch out — people close to you can be unpredictable at times. Now is a good time to start planning a long break away from it all but don't rush into things. Saturn is moving into retrograde this week which could mean a downturn in fortunes both emotional and financial, so try and devote some time to any worries before things get out of hand. Play safe this week and don't take any unnecessary risks. Above all, beware of rash decisions!

CHAPTER ONE

'I'm going to lunch, Jo. Do you want anything?' Celia popped her head round the door, freshly lipsticked and beaming underneath a frosting of curly white hair.

Jo muted her phone. 'Have we got enough coffee?'

'Plenty, but I'll get some more. Some of that vile continental blend you like.'

'Not decaffeinated,' Jo called as Celia's head disappeared. In her ear, she heard the voice of the HR advisor from the NHS Trust returning to the phone. He was full of apologies for keeping her waiting and confirmed that a certain Lee Kwok had worked at Dudley Road Hospital as a general nurse between 2012 and 2018, which was just the information Jo was looking for. She thanked him and flicked back to the copy of Lee Kwok's application form. Yes, Ms Kwok had been telling the truth. Next to check her date of birth: Lee Kwok was a Capricorn, which meant she passed Jo's own private selection procedure and her completed form went on the left-hand pile.

This was one of the better jobs Jo had been given since she had started work at Macy and Wilson as a part-time PI. A private hospital was opening in Coventry and the new director had asked the agency to verify the references of shortlisted applicants. Jo's boss, David Macy, had passed the job on to her and she had added her own twist to the process. She was putting aside the forms of applicants born under Virgo and Capricorn and was intending to advise the director that these people would make the best nurses — according to astrological wisdom, anyway.

Jo picked up the last form and looked at it without enthusiasm. She had been doing the same job all morning and was finding it difficult to concentrate. She could hear Celia's high heels clattering down the stairs to the front door. It was very warm — summer had well and truly arrived — and the office was stuffy. This dark, poky room doubled up as a kitchen for the few staff at the agency and had one small window. Jo got up to look out, peering down at the backs of shops in the alley below.

Working as a part-time PI may have its tedious moments but Jo had found she was surprisingly good at it. She had a certain amount of audacity combined with dogged perseverance. Anyway, she could put up with the more boring days because, she reminded herself, it was only temporary work until she could become a full-time astrologer. Her real passion was casting charts for people. Payment for astrological advice plus her weekly horoscope column for a local paper and wages from Macy meant she had just enough to live on. But even with the two jobs, her landlord still had to wait a couple of weeks for the rent now and again. And her mother moaned that she would never 'settle down with a mortgage'.

Jo turned back to the unfinished application form on her desk, but it still did not appeal, and she wandered out looking for coffee. There was none brewing in the reception area where Celia worked so Jo looked around for something else to divert her. It was unusual for her to have the whole place to herself. According to Celia, Macy had gone to Sheffield for the day and Jo, trying the door to his office, found it open. She had half-expected it to be locked, knowing how jealously he guarded his privacy.

The cluttered, dusty room was not much better than the one she had just left. She opened both windows, sat in Macy's old, comfortable office chair and looked at the papers spread out on the desk. He had obviously taken the laptop and neither they nor the room revealed much about Macy except he wasn't very tidy and didn't spend any money on office furniture. She knew remarkably little about him and, irritatingly, this made him more attractive.

Swivelling round in her chair, she regarded the old-fashioned filing cabinets behind her. They were unlabelled and probably full of work files as Macy had not exactly embraced the paperless office. She tried a few of the metal drawers and discovered she was right. In the cabinet closest to the door she opened a folder containing some letters signed by Mark Wilson. Though the agency was called Macy and Wilson, no one had ever mentioned who Wilson was. Even Celia couldn't be drawn on the subject.

So he did exist then, Jo thought. These letters were six years old, and looking back further in the file, she found one from an accountant, which listed three partners of Macy and Wilson: Mark Wilson, David Macy and Jill Macy. Now who was that — his sister or, more likely, his wife? He lived on his own in the flat above the office so he must be divorced now. But why all the secrecy?

While she was delving into another file, Jo heard someone moving about in the outer office. She put the file back together and tried to peer through the frosted glass door. Theoretically clients could drop in to the agency but this did not happen often and it was unlike Celia to forget an appointment. Someone was standing in the other room. Jo hoped it wasn't Macy. She was still struggling with the filing cabinet when there was a gentle tap on the glass.

'Come in,' Jo called, and a man walked in, looking around with an air of hopeful enquiry. He was young, smart and slightly flushed from the heat. His reddish cheeks clashed with the straw colour of his hair, Jo noticed, but his expression was open and confident.

'Ms Macy or Ms Wilson?' He gave her a smile and held out his hand.

'Neither,' Jo explained, managing finally to shove the cabinet drawer closed, 'I'm Jo Hughes. Mr Macy is out on business today. And Mr Wilson has — er — left the firm.' She took his proffered hand and he gave hers a single practised shake across the desk. There didn't seem much point in explaining that she had only borrowed the office so she offered him one of the battered old leather chairs Macy kept for clients.

'Connor Fitzpatrick.' He handed her a business card. His narrow blue eyes flickered around the room from under a sharp, styled haircut, albeit slightly frizzy due to the hot day. He appeared to be taking in the ordered clutter of Macy's office. 'I've never actually been to a private investigation agency before,' he said with a disarming smile.

'How can we help, Mr Fitzpatrick?' Jo wondered what Macy would want to know about this man. Fitzpatrick's card didn't tell her much. It was from a London firm of stockbrokers, about which she knew nothing.

He took a breath and leaned forward, placing his palms together. 'Well, do you look for missing people? Because my brother has gone missing and it's difficult to get the police to take it seriously.'

'How long has he been gone?' Jo asked. She had been thinking how attractive Fitzpatrick was but now firmly redirected her thoughts.

'Nearly two weeks.' Fitzpatrick gave Jo a look that tried to anticipate her reaction. 'I suppose you think that's not long and I'm being a bit overprotective?'

She shook her head. 'Have you thought he might have been in an accident?' she asked, as delicately as she could.

'I've rung round all the hospitals. Thank God, he's not there.' Fitzpatrick paused, looking exasperated. 'The police said that too, and advised me to give it a month and go back to them if I still hadn't heard from him. But I know something's wrong.'

‘If you could tell me a bit more about his disappearance . . . ?’

‘All right,’ he agreed. Fitzpatrick’s self-assurance was obvious. He gave himself time to collect his thoughts, then spoke matter-of-factly again. ‘Sean is thirty — that’s four years younger than me. He works for a bank and he’s doing reasonably well at it. But he’s very bright and could probably do a lot better if he wanted to. We share a house in Putney — we bought it two years ago — and although we don’t exactly live in each other’s pockets, I usually know roughly where he is.’

‘Go on.’

‘OK, a week last Friday he went off to the office as usual. I saw him at breakfast. We didn’t say much but we never do at that time of day. We’re both owls not larks, if you know what I mean. He seemed just the same as ever. He took a small holdall with him but I thought that was sports stuff. He drove off in his car as if he was going to work as normal. I found out later he’d booked that day off work but he didn’t turn up at the office when he was supposed to on the Monday. Now, ten days later, there’s been no word from him — not a text or message, nothing posted on Facebook and his phone is dead as a dodo.’ After Fitzpatrick had presented these facts, he sat back and waited for Jo’s reaction.

She had been scribbling down some of this in a notepad she found on Macy’s desk. ‘We do take on cases like this,’ she said with more confidence than she felt. She found a rate sheet and handed it over to him. ‘We would bill you for our time, plus expenses. But first, I’d need to know a bit more — like where exactly your brother works?’

‘At the National Commercial Bank at London Bridge. Do you know London well?’

Jo paused in her note-taking and looked up. ‘Yes, a bit — but if Sean lives and works in London, what are you doing in Coventry?’

‘Well, I’ve started to do my own detective work.’ A brief boyish smile flitted across his face. ‘I know Sean came here on the eighteenth of June because I found his last bank statement and he made a cash withdrawal from a bank in Coventry.'

'Do you know what he was doing here?'

Fitzpatrick shook his head. 'Maybe something to do with a woman — I've noticed a new voice on his messages at the house lately.'

'A girlfriend?' Jo felt like she was building up a picture of Sean using babies' building blocks. But it was a start.

'Probably. He hasn't had a regular—' Fitzpatrick paused over the word — 'relationship for a while. But I think he was seeing someone new called Rosie. Knowing Sean, it wouldn't be anything serious.'

'Do you know how to get in touch with her?' Jo asked.

Fitzpatrick shook his head.

'You said you've had messages from her? Where are they? On your home phone?'

'Yes, she left the odd message for him, which I picked up. Nothing very unusual about that but I just noticed it was a new name. Sean's car is still missing as well, by the way. I should have mentioned that.' He gave the make and registration and Jo scribbled this down. This case appealed to her. It was fascinating to think that someone could just write themselves out of their own lives. It looked to her as if that's exactly what Fitzpatrick's brother had done.

'Has he been depressed lately?'

'No — he's not a moody person. He's been his usual easy-going self.' Fitzpatrick seemed to accept all her questions with the same open-faced equilibrium.

'Do you know what he took with him?'

'I've looked in his room and it's difficult to say. All his clothes seem to be there. I found his passport, so he didn't take that. He had his credit cards and wallet and his phone on him of course. He left his laptop and I can get into that, but I can't find anything much on there.' He frowned for the first time, a line appearing on his smooth forehead. 'And I think he took some overnight stuff — his shaver was missing.'

'Have you thought he might not want to be found?' Jo asked. 'People do just decide to take off, I'm afraid.'

Fitzpatrick shook his head soberly. 'It's possible but even if he has, I want to know where he is.' He didn't expand on this but his mind was clearly made up and Jo knew Macy would not want her to talk a client out of employing them.

'All right, then. We'll see what we can do,' Jo heard herself say. She wondered if Macy would mind that his most junior and newest employee had just taken on a case.

She paused before asking any more questions and tried to imagine what she would do if her sister Marie went missing. She would be worried, of course, but she would also be superfluous because her parents and Marie's husband would be heading the chase to find her.

That was a point. 'Are your parents alive?' Jo asked. 'Do they have any idea where he might be?'

'No, none at all.' Fitzpatrick was dismissive. 'And I don't know any of his friends all that well. I asked some discreet questions at the bank where he works but that didn't help. I'm glad you'll take this on anyway,' he added. He had a habit of giving a little, affirming nod as if to reinforce his point. 'I've realised there's a limit to what I can do on my own. I've been up here all morning and got nowhere.'

'What have you tried?' Jo asked.

'I asked at his bank to see if they could tell me what time he withdrew the money from the cash machine on the eighteenth but they wouldn't, no matter how high up the hierarchy I went. It was more than the manager's job was worth I think.'

That would explain why he'd set out on the hottest day of the year dressed for the boardroom, Jo thought. She took down the name and address of the local bank and made a mental note to mention this to Macy. It was quite possible that he'd know someone at the bank who would divulge this information.

'Then I went round the hospitals here,' Fitzpatrick was saying. 'I'd already tried the obvious London ones. But he's got to be somewhere, hasn't he? And I can't understand why he hasn't got in touch.'

'We'll do what we can.' Jo realised she was smiling back at the handsome, slightly frazzled man opposite her. Just last year she would have been amazed at herself for taking on such a job. It had nothing to do with astrology, which was meant to be her real business and she had a sudden, guilty sense that her friend Hanni, the crystal healer, would not approve. *You don't want to disperse your energies and invite darkness into your life, Jo*, she would say. Or something like that anyway. She brushed away the thought. 'Do you have a photograph of your brother?'

She wondered what Sean was like. It seemed likely he was in some sort of trouble. Or had he just left a boring job to run off with his girlfriend? Most importantly, when was he born?

Connor Fitzpatrick handed over his phone, showing a decent head-and-shoulders photograph of his brother — a solid, square man who appeared to be standing, arms folded, on the drive of a large house. He was fair like Connor but broader and stockier and his face was a different shape: wider and squarer, with the hint of a beard along his fleshy jawline. His expression was more inscrutable but also, oddly, more bland. His light eyes regarded the camera with a bored expression below springy hair, equally well-styled. He was certainly not as attractive as his younger brother but appeared just as confident.

Fitzpatrick was looking at Jo curiously. 'I'm going to say something now, which you might think a bit rude of me but, you know, you seem a bit young to be running a place like this. I hope you don't mind my mentioning—'

'Oh, I don't run it.' Jo laughed and handed back his phone. She explained that it was just a part-time job while she tried to establish her own business as an astrologer.

Fitzpatrick's eyebrows rose and he leaned forward. 'Really? You can cast charts and say how people will be feeling next week? Is that it?'

This was as accurate a description of an astrologer's work as she had heard from a layperson and Jo was impressed. Most people tended to be superior about it, which was very irritating. 'It could be useful in finding out what's happened to your brother,' she suggested. 'I could draw up Sean's natal chart for you, if you like, and from that it would be possible to know if he was going through a difficult time around the eighteenth.'

Fitzpatrick was enthusiastic and said he would get back to her with the details she would need about Sean's exact time of birth. 'But I can tell you straight away he's a Taurus. Does that help?'

'It surprises me,' Jo admitted. 'Taureans don't usually make radical, sudden changes in their lives as a rule. They go for security and routine and navigate change very much at their own pace. If your brother just upped and went of his own accord, something must have made him willing to sacrifice all that.' She also knew that Saturn had just moved into retrograde in Taurus, which meant it was not a good time for them to unnecessary risks but she kept this to herself.

Fitzpatrick was shaking his head. 'It doesn't sound like Sean — what you say about him choosing the safe options. He likes security in the form of money well enough but he likes to take a few risks too, if you know what I mean. He has always been a bit of a daredevil — so I'm not that convinced by astrology so far.' He softened this remark with an appealing smile.

'You can't tell much from just his Sun Sign. That's the kind of thing that will come out in his chart,' Jo explained. 'I'll tell you more when I've worked it out if you let me have his birth time, precise to within fifteen minutes, the date and location.'

Fitzpatrick happily agreed to pay for this additional work. Money was no problem, clearly. 'Thanks for this.' He offered his hand. 'I'm glad I looked you up. I'll email you with the other details so you can just send me the bills. And will you ring me to keep in touch?'

Jo shook on her first PI business. 'Yes, I'd want to come down to London,' she said, 'ask some questions at his office and generally find out a bit more about Sean.'

'I'll give you the bank's number.' Fitzpatrick produced a fountain pen and turned her notebook around to face him. 'That will save you some time. His manager's name is Walmsley — this is his direct line. But I'd rather you didn't mention Sean's disappearance to anyone there. When he comes back to take up the reins, he might prefer them to think he'd been ill. I'll send you the address of our house in Putney, too. And this is my phone number in case you think of anything else to ask me about Sean.' He wrote down the two numbers with something of a flourish.

'Thanks.' Jo stood up to show Fitzpatrick out. 'One thing — what about your Sun Sign? What are you?'

'Can't you guess?' he grinned.

Jo had expected this. The way he was constantly shifting his position and using his hands when he spoke, while his eyes wandered restlessly around the room gave him away as a Gemini. He also had that strange mixture of diffidence and confidence, which she had observed in other Geminis. She was often attracted to Geminis and Fitzpatrick was another example: she liked the easy way he talked and she had the feeling that he couldn't be serious for long. In fact, he probably couldn't be anything for long. She was about to make a confident guess when the door of the office opened and Macy walked in.

He stopped and looked around with an air of mild surprise. With his dark eyes and hair, jeans and loud summer shirt, he stood out in contrast to the neat, fair Fitzpatrick. Macy always had a slightly cynical air, which made the difference between the two men even more marked. Jo suspected he was not pleased to find her installed behind his desk, particularly because she was talking to a client who was younger than him and better looking. As Macy was a Cancerian, it wouldn't matter to him that he had no justification or excuse to be jealous.

'I'm sorry, I didn't realise my office was engaged,' Macy said. She was not deceived — the very pleasantness of his tone signified a sulk in the offing and his words were accompanied with a hard look at Jo. Fitzpatrick appeared blissfully unaware of the sins that had been committed and simply waited for Jo to introduce him, which she did. She explained briefly about the case. Macy nodded encouragingly, miming rapt attention. Jo thought he was overdoing it slightly. When she had finished, he turned his attention to Fitzpatrick. 'Have you tried the Missing Persons' Unit and the Salvation Army? And the local police here?'

Fitzpatrick shook his head.

'OK, that's where we can start then. Can I get you a coffee?'

'I was just about to go,' Fitzpatrick put in. 'Jo has been extremely helpful and she seems to have it all under control.'

'That's nice,' Macy said with his most charming smile. Jo duly led Fitzpatrick out, leaving Macy to reclaim his office. There was only one way to deal with Macy in a bad mood, Jo had learned, and that was to go on the attack straight away.

'I got you some business there,' she said brightly when she went back into his office. Macy was ostentatiously moving things around on his desk as if they had been disturbed by a hurricane.

'Hmm. What about the reference checking?' he said, lining up his notepad and pen.

'I'll finish it at home. Is there anything you want to know about that man Fitzpatrick before I go?'

'No.' Macy gave her a brief look but as usual his eyes gave nothing away and he became deeply absorbed in setting up his laptop. 'I'll put Alan on the case. And you can leave the notes behind too.'

Jo placed the sheet of notepaper on his desk. 'Oh well, suit yourself,' she said. 'I have to go now. I'm going to London this evening.'

Once outside, she was annoyed that she had allowed herself to descend to Macy's childish level. Sometimes she said what she thought when she knew she would be better off keeping quiet: that was her Sagittarian Ascendant. She should have retained the moral high ground and calmly voiced her objections to his giving Alan the case. She had won it, she felt, and she deserved it. She would have enjoyed finding out more about Sean Fitzpatrick's disappearance. And some more about his brother too, come to that. Connor Fitzpatrick had aroused in Jo an interesting mixture of attraction and suspicion.

She stopped her thoughts in their tracks. Maybe it was not a bad thing after all if she didn't get any further involved in this case. She didn't want to get mixed up with any unreliable Geminis.

CHAPTER TWO

Jo had done all the research work she ever needed on attractive male Geminis. In fact she was meeting one that evening. She and Tim had lived together years ago when she had been working for a newspaper in Wales and Tim was a student. She had thought he was totally committed until she discovered he had been giving the A-Level student he saw on Tuesday nights more than just special maths tuition. Jo had forgotten the Gemini facility to do two things at once. Nowadays she and Tim were purely platonic and it was more relaxing. He was still a student but now living in London and she often stayed at his flat.

Connor Fitzpatrick's boyish charm had reminded her of Tim and she told herself she should steer clear. All the same she couldn't help feeling pleased when the case was unexpectedly handed back to her. She was battling to dry her curly shoulder-length hair a couple of hours later when Alan rang. Since leaving the office she had been for a swim, which had a positive effect on her mood but inevitably a bad effect on her hair.

'Jo, I want you to do me a favour.' Alan's voice was even more brusque than usual over the phone and he wasted no time on pleasantries. 'Did Macy tell you about this missing Irish bloke I'm supposed to be looking for?'

Jo admitted she knew all about it.

'I've got a snowball's chance in hell of finding him,' he moaned. 'Does Macy realise that?'

'I know there wasn't much to go on. Just a woman called Rosie who might or might not live in Coventry and a date two weeks ago when he took cash out of his bank account. But you could check there first to see if that actually happened. Otherwise this man may never have even come to Coventry.'

'I suppose it might be worth a try.' Alan was sceptical. 'Listen, Macy says you're going to London tonight. Are you? Because he wants me to go down too.'

Jo almost groaned aloud. She usually managed to tolerate him very well, despite disagreeing about nearly everything, but Alan was still only bearable in small doses. She was looking forward to her evening: she intended to go to a lecture held by the Astrological Society and stay at Tim's overnight. Alan didn't fit into these plans. But it turned out he had no desire to savour the delights of the capital.

'I hate the place,' he said. 'Don't know why so many people put up with working there. You used to, though, didn't you? You must know your way around? Are you staying over?'

'What do you want me to do?' Jo put down her hairdryer and sat down.

'It won't take long,' he promised. 'Macy wants me to go and see the missing bloke's parents. They won't speak to me on the phone. I was going to pop into the bank where he works as well but you might not have time for that. I'll give you a share of the pay of course.'

'OK. I will need Connor's phone number. And—' an idea occurred to her — 'maybe you could do something for me in return. You know about cars, don't you?' She knew he did, even though he drove an ancient, grimy estate car. One of Alan's many jobs before joining the agency had been a mechanic. Jo had bought her Renault a week ago and it had started making an ominous knocking noise. She asked if Alan would have a look at it.

‘Any time you like. Foreign-built of course,’ he added cheerfully before ringing off. ‘Told you to buy British-made, didn’t I?’

Jo rolled her eyes at the phone but she had to admit she felt a modicum of satisfaction that Alan had dropped the Fitzpatrick case back into her lap. She guessed Macy would not be pleased. Going back to her make-up mirror, she gave herself a conspiratorial smile, which faded when she noticed her still-damp hair. She had failed to tame it into good behaviour. It was wavy and dark and difficult, in her opinion. She had inherited it from her father, who described himself as a Welsh–Italian, although he had moved to Coventry before Jo was born. Jo’s eyes were grey like her father’s and she liked to think she had something of a pale and interesting Celtic look. But she could have done without the abundant hair.

Due to the conversation with Alan, she ended up rushing to the station. She couldn’t trust her car on long journeys at the moment. Once on the train with a cup of coffee slopping around in front of her, she opened her laptop and her astrology app. Just knowing Sean Fitzpatrick’s date of birth was enough to tell her the position of the planets on the day he was born. It gave her a starting point but no more. As she had told Connor, she would need to know exactly when and where he was born before she could draw up his natal chart.

Sean had three important planets in Aries, which would certainly make him more selfish, decisive and quick-tempered than the average Taurean. And Venus was in Pisces, which meant he was excitable and easily bored. Not a typical contented Taurus at all, Jo thought, and she itched to be able to delve into the rest of his chart.

As she couldn’t, she went over the story Connor Fitzpatrick had told her. She thought of it as a story because she didn’t entirely believe it. But it must at least be true that his brother had disappeared, and that was what interested her. Why would someone just up and go like that? Was he running from or to something? And what had prompted him to leave on that particular morning?

CHAPTER THREE

As a member of the Astrological Society, Jo was entitled to attend the monthly lectures at the college in Bloomsbury and she often managed to make it. Tonight an expert on horary astrology was speaking and Jo didn't entirely agree with him.

'You can cast a chart to answer any question,' the lecturer said, throwing his arms expansively. 'By assuming the question comes into being the moment it is asked, it is possible to deduce the answer from the planets.'

Jo was dubious. Like most astrologers, she didn't believe astrology could predict the future in specific terms. If it was as easy as that, she could tell from the position of the planets what exactly had been on Sean's mind the moment he left the house on that Friday morning. She decided she should stick to analysing his natal chart because she knew she could do that well.

After the lecture she spent the rest of the evening with Tim, who wanted to tell her all about his differences of opinion with his tutor. So it wasn't until the following day when she was on the Tube heading east across London that she was able to give Sean Fitzpatrick the concentration he deserved. She balanced a new notebook on her knee and tried to reconstruct the notes she had left at Macy's. The fact that no one at the office apart from Alan knew she was working on the case gave her free rein to tackle it any way she liked and she enjoyed that feeling.

Sean Fitzpatrick's office was in the city in one of those narrow roads where office blocks of different decades are squashed uneasily together. It took some finding, which Jo had not anticipated. She had thought the headquarters of a big clearing bank like the National Commercial would be more imposing than the anonymous ten-storey building she eventually found.

It took a minute for her eyes to adjust from the bright sunlight outside to the dim interior. She successfully negotiated her way past the dark glass coffee tables and black leather seats to the desk at the back, where a woman watched her progress expectantly from behind a spot-lit desk. Probably this woman's sole entertainment was watching temporarily blinded people crash into plate-glass tables, Jo thought.

'Have you an appointment?' the woman asked in cool tones.

'I've come to see Sean Fitzpatrick.'

'What section?'

'I'm sorry, I don't know.'

The woman consulted a list and then looked up at Jo with an understanding smile. 'Oh yes — the interviews. I'll let them know you're here.'

Jo started to say that no one was expecting her but the woman had turned away to make a call. Jo had only come to the bank in a bid to understand more about Sean for herself, rather than just hearing it from his brother. She had not expected to get even this far into his place of work but she had learned it was better sometimes to let events take their course. She sat on one of the leather chairs and sank so deeply she couldn't see how she was going to get up without displaying her upper thighs to the world. After a minute or two, the woman came over with some papers. She looked surprisingly normal without her desk.

‘You’re a little early, they said. Mr Walmsley will send someone down for you in about twenty minutes.’

‘What about Mr Fitzpatrick?’ Jo asked, all innocence. ‘I specifically came to see him.’

‘I’m afraid he’s not in today. Don’t worry, Mr Walmsley is from the same section.’

Jo thanked her and wondered what she was getting into. *Well, perhaps it’s time I had a career change*, she thought. She wished she had picked up a coffee on her way in to help pass the time.

Soon enough a well-groomed man of about her own age appeared from the lift opposite and came over to her. He introduced himself as Vaz Harri. ‘Follow me, I’ll show you around. We are seeing about thirty people today and hope to get a shortlist for a formal interview next week. I see you have not worked in customer service before?’

Jo had to admit this was true but she had done various office jobs and said so as she followed Vaz into the lift. He asked her about them in a friendly, laconic manner as they travelled up to the ninth floor and through an open-plan office. She walked between groups of desks, past people staring at their screens in a hushed atmosphere not unlike a library. No one glanced in their direction. She remembered, not with any nostalgia, the strange, enclosed world of office life.

Jo hurried to catch up with Vaz’s long strides and fell into step at his side. ‘Do you know Sean Fitzpatrick?’ she asked.

‘Yes, he works here—’ Vaz nodded towards an office door — ‘but he’s not in today. Why? Do you know him?’

‘Yes, he told me about the job,’ Jo said.

‘Oh, did he?’ Vaz turned to her with a piercing gaze. ‘You should have as good a chance as anybody, in that case.’

Jo wondered what that was supposed to mean. ‘Is he off sick, then?’ she persevered.

‘As far as I know,’ Vaz said in a tone which did not welcome further questions. He led her to a couple of sofas in the corporate colours of grey and maroon. They were placed opposite each other inside a booth with soft walls made of the same material, which gave the impression of being soundproof. *Although I wouldn't want to share any secrets in here*, Jo thought as she took a seat opposite Vaz.

He sat down and spread out some papers on the low table in front of him. 'I'll tell you a bit about the job now.'

Jo listened as he launched into an explanation of the vacancy, which he probably had to repeat thirty times that day. It seemed to be straightforward temporary office work, involving answering customer enquiries and keeping a note of their questions on record. They were launching a new savings scheme and were expecting a glut of calls. Jo listened and dutifully answered his questions about her experience while she also took the opportunity to look around her. This was an unexpected insight into Connor's brother's work life and she wanted to glean every little detail that she could.

It was a quiet corner of the floor, with no phones ringing. Not far away were glass offices, like mini goldfish bowls. Some were occupied and she wondered if one of them might belong to Sean. Jo would have dearly liked to take a look in there.

'Do you enjoy working here?' she asked Vaz when he seemed to have come to the end of his set questions.

Vaz hesitated. 'Of course,' he answered. He bit his top lip, suddenly seeming less assured, which made him appear younger.

'A lot of people don't like their jobs,' she said with a little explanatory shrug. 'Is this a good place to work? Things going on socially?'

'Oh yes.' Vaz gave a relieved smile. 'We go out as a team sometimes for meals or pub quizzes. Donna, over there—' he nodded his head towards a middle-aged woman who was writing on a whiteboard — 'you want to talk to her if you want the social calendar. She organises all of us — even Mr Fitzpatrick and Mr Walmsley — and makes them join in.'

'And you all get on well?' Jo asked. 'Even with the bosses?'

'Very well,' Vaz replied. 'Nick Walmsley is great to work for—'

‘What about Sean?’ Jo asked and tried to soften the question by adding, ‘Some bosses are so difficult, aren’t they?’

‘He’s very friendly too,’ Vaz answered but his sharp eyes were regarding her suspiciously.

Jo felt there was a certain constraint in this reply but there were no chances to find out any more until Vaz showed her out. When they were travelling down in the lift, Jo asked him how well he knew Sean Fitzpatrick. She felt she had nothing to lose now. Vaz looked at her with open curiosity.

‘I wish I knew why you are so interested in him,’ he commented.

Jo wondered how much she should tell him. ‘What do you mean?’

‘Well, let’s put it like this,’ Vaz said as the lift came to a smooth halt. ‘If your interest is professional, then you should ask someone more on his level. I’m just a minion,’ he added with a small, self-deprecating smile. ‘If it is personal . . .’ He stepped out of the lift.

‘Go on.’ Jo followed him through the dim foyer.

When they had walked a few paces past the reception desk, Vaz looked at her. ‘If you were a friend of mine and you were thinking of being interested in him personally,’ he said, ‘I would say don’t, that’s all.’ He stopped at the front doors and shrugged his shoulders. ‘You probably won’t take my advice anyway.’

‘I’m not sure I understand it,’ Jo said, wanting him to explain further.

Vaz smiled and pushed the glass door open for her. ‘You do,’ he said. ‘We will be in touch on the number you gave and who knows? Maybe I will see you again soon.’

Jo stepped out into the street, blinking again. *Well, that was something and nothing,* she thought. *Now for lunch.*

CHAPTER FOUR

Jo bought some peanut butter and banana sandwiches and ate them on the train to Richmond. Sitting in a half-empty carriage with the window down, she thought about Vaz. She had instinctively liked him. She had decided he was probably a Virgo like herself and she had taken to him because he seemed efficient, reserved and not one to suffer fools gladly.

Pity she couldn't have got more out of him about Sean, she reflected, but it was difficult to ask searching questions when she had promised Connor not to mention that his brother had disappeared. Vaz had hinted that Sean Fitzpatrick was bad news for women. Something Connor Fitzpatrick had said had given Jo a similar impression. But this was not enlightening. *After all, what man isn't?* she thought in a cynical moment. Maybe Sean's parents would help to flesh out his character.

The Fitzpatricks lived just off Richmond Hill, on a quiet road where most of the houses looked deceptively ordinary. Jo guessed they actually belonged to media types and orthodontists. Alan had given her the address and she found the place easily enough using her phone and the map at the station. This meant she was walking up the drive by four o'clock, which she reckoned was pretty good going. The house was a square, symmetrical Georgian building of pale brick and long windows, and something about the place gave her a sense of *déjà vu*. As she rang the tastefully quiet doorbell, the reason came to her. In his photograph, Sean Fitzpatrick had been standing on this same pink gravel drive.

A middle-aged woman opened the door just wide enough for her to see out with dignity. She wore a suit in expensive, dingy colours and looked at Jo with a vague distrust, not quite hidden by a thin smile.

'Mrs Fitzpatrick?' Jo asked tentatively. She felt that anyone who could afford to live in a house as grand as this would be unlikely to open the door themselves. But she was wrong. The older woman nodded and continued to look at Jo cautiously.

'I was speaking to your son yesterday—'

'Which one?' Mrs Fitzpatrick asked.

'Connor. He said you might be able to help. He's very concerned about Sean. Do you mind if I come in?' Jo hoped to get inside the house. Interviews on doorsteps were hopeless. People were always distracted and preoccupied and their means of escape was too accessible.

'I won't be able to tell you anything about Sean's whereabouts,' Mrs Fitzpatrick said. Her sandy eyebrows drew together in a discouraging frown. 'Are you another of the private investigators Connor has hired? I had one rude individual ring me up last night.'

'It won't take long, honestly,' Jo said with false cheerfulness, hoping to gloss over Alan's misdemeanours. 'If I could just come in—'

Mrs Fitzpatrick grudgingly agreed, specifying that she only had ten minutes to spare. Jo, silently victorious, followed the tall woman down her spacious hall. She had a slim build and a conscious grace: even her high heels tapped a well-modulated rhythm on the shiny parquet. Her clothes and make-up were immaculate. Jo scrutinised both as Mrs Fitzpatrick opened a door to let Jo walk ahead of her into a well-furnished, comfortable sitting room. It was her bone structure that made the woman look so striking. She had the same high cheek bones and deep, narrow eyes as Connor. With that willowy figure, Jo guessed that she had been gorgeous not so long ago.

'Will you sit down?' Mrs Fitzpatrick asked with formal politeness. 'I'm Fiona Fitzpatrick, by the way. You are?'

Jo introduced herself and sat down on a chair covered in a bold, striped fabric. The room, at the back of the house, smelled faintly of dried flowers and polish. It seemed to be used partly as an office except the desk was a large fancy bureau and the computer was on a cherrywood dining-table. Hardly standard office furniture, Jo thought. The windows were heavily draped, which made it dark. Mrs Fitzpatrick did not sit but leaned against the table, where her discreet bottom gently dislodged some papers from a pile.

Jo watched as a single page floated to the carpet. Fiona Fitzpatrick did not bother to pick it up. 'When did you last see Sean?'

'About a month ago. He came for Sunday lunch, which he does once a month.' She sighed. 'I hope Connor knows what he's doing. I don't really see how you can help.'

'It is mainly what we do: tracing people. We are good at it.' This woman's superior air made Jo feel defensive. 'The police won't do much about a missing person if there are no suspicious circumstances. Connor seems to be very worried about his brother—'

'Yes, he does, doesn't he?' Fiona Fitzpatrick gave Jo a look of amused tolerance like someone watching a sport she doesn't understand. 'Why do you think that is?' she asked, continuing to look at Jo. 'Or don't you ask yourselves questions like that if someone is paying the bill?'

Jo ignored the question. 'Are *you* worried about your son, Mrs Fitzpatrick?'

'I gave up wondering if he had a hot dinner and a clean shirt long before he left home and that was more than ten years ago.' Jo noticed the slight Irish accent for the first time. Mrs Fitzpatrick ostentatiously consulted her watch and Jo felt she must plough on with her questions. She knew so little about Sean, virtually any question would do.

'Did he leave home to share a house with Connor?'

'No, Connor was at Oxford then. Sean left to get married and settle down.' Mrs Fitzpatrick finished on a laugh.

Jo failed to see the joke. 'He's not married anymore?'

'No,' came the short answer.

'Can you let me have the name and address of his ex-wife?'

'She was called Valerie. I have no idea where she is now.'

Jo made a mental note to ask Connor. 'Where do you think Sean might be?' she tried.

Fiona Fitzpatrick pulled at a long silver pendant around her neck and her large eyes settled on a space past Jo. She shrugged elegantly. 'Sydney? Rio? The Orkneys? Your guess is as good as mine. Now I must remind you, I said a few minutes only. I have to ask you to go.' She gave the impression of someone who had done their painful duty. Smug and indifferent would be the two words to choose between, Jo thought, if she were asked to sum up the woman in one.

'I suppose you remember him being born?' Jo stood up, glancing round the room and taking in the expensive clutter.

'Sorry?' Fiona Fitzpatrick sounded gratifyingly puzzled by the change of tack.

Jo went over to a waist-high urn of dried flowers in the hearth as if drawn to the arrangement. In fact, she had noticed some family photographs on the mantelpiece and wanted to get a discreet look. 'Lovely display,' she said.

'What do you mean about remembering Sean's birth?' the woman asked, allowing a querulous note into her voice.

'I know he's not the eldest, but do you remember him being born?' The photographs were all dull studio portraits of various family members. Jo picked out the ones she knew. Connor was there, his pointed chin and sexy blue eyes looking ingenuously over his mother's shoulder. She recognised Sean, standing straight, uncompromising and none-too-cheerful between what must be his father and elder brother. They were both well-built and swarthy and noticeably father and son.

'I think it's really time for you to go—' Fiona Fitzpatrick's heels were tapping towards the door.

'Yes,' Jo agreed. 'I just wondered if you could tell me when Sean was born. The exact birth time and place, if possible.' Jo turned to face the other woman and smiled politely, adding that she was an astrologer and had promised to cast Sean's horoscope.

Fiona sighed. 'I despair of Connor, I really do.' Making it obvious she thought the whole idea was nonsense, she nevertheless gave the necessary information. Jo noted it down, tempted to ask for Connor's details too, but decided not to push her luck.

'What about your husband, could he help me?' Jo said, taking her time on her journey down the hall to the front door.

'I don't think you would want to wait for him. He will not be home until eleven tonight,' Mrs Fitzpatrick said, adding quietly, 'if then.'

'Perhaps I could see him at work?' Jo felt it was worth a try. She stopped in front of a sombre watercolour in the hall.

'Oh yes, he would love a chat about his favourite son over the operating table.'

The older woman's sarcasm was a little heavy, Jo thought. 'Your husband's a doctor?'

'A consultant.' Mrs Fitzpatrick stepped past Jo and opened the front door. 'But I really don't advise you to contact him. He has even less interest in this business than I do.'

It was the nearest Jo had ever come to being thrown out and as she pounded back down the hill towards the station, she found herself feeling cross about it. Fiona Fitzpatrick had so obviously looked down her nose. Even if the woman couldn't give a damn if her son was alive or dead, there was no need to be so rude. Her superciliousness grated far more than a string of insults would have done and gradually, waiting for the train, Jo began to feel annoyed with Connor Fitzpatrick as well. After all, if he was going to employ private investigators to find his brother, you would think he could at least persuade his mother to be civil to them.

By the time her train had stopped at Putney, curiosity about seeing Connor again had overcome her irritation. His narrow, terraced house was not far from the station but when she rang the intercom beside the shiny grey door, there was no answer. She stood in the brick storm porch and looked up and down the street. There were plenty of people about but no sign of Connor.

She looked at her watch. It was only half past five and she realised he would probably still be at work. Of course, she could call him to find out but, instinctively, she had wanted to surprise him with a visit. To drop in on him, rather as he had dropped into the office in Coventry. If he was still at work, she could catch him at his office and surprise him there, she mused, or just wait for him to come home. He could be hours, though. She tried the doorbell again. The black venetian blinds behind the bay window meant that she could not see inside.

After waiting a few more minutes, she dug out her phone. She had left Connor's business card in Macy's office and had only asked Alan for Connor's personal number. However, she remembered the name of the company and it didn't take her long to look up their number. When she called and asked to speak to Connor, a man told her he had left for the day.

If Connor came straight home, he would be here soon. She wandered down Putney high street and selected a pizzeria to get the cup of coffee she had been craving since lunchtime. She concluded that it was worth waiting as long as it took to drink a coffee. After that, she might have to give up the surprise element of her plan and just give him a call. Her spirits were improved by the dose of caffeine and she felt another lift as she walked back up Chiltern Street and saw a new black Peugeot outside Connor's house that had not been there before. She rang the doorbell confidently. Beside her, she noticed the blinds shudder and then Connor, looking more rumpled than when she had last seen him, with his tie loose and his shoes in his hands, came to the door.

'Jo!' He sounded pleased to see her. 'Are you on the case? Have you come to interrogate me? Come in and have a drink.'

He's more hospitable than his mother, anyway. Jo smiled at Connor and, feeling how easy it was to succumb to his obvious charm, had to remind herself that she was annoyed with him.

'I was just fixing myself a teeny little gin. How about you?' Connor led the way into the front room.

Jo accepted the offer of a drink and took a seat on an impractically white sofa while he went to get it. The room was austere and monochrome. The minimalist style, apart from being dated, did not go with the house. She picked up some envelopes on the sofa beside her — just bills and circulars. They didn't tell her any more about Connor or Sean than the room did.

'So have you come to give me a progress report, or what?' Connor handed her a heavy glass, which clinked with ice. 'What have you found? Any clue as to where he is?' He sat down on a very uncomfortable-looking swivel armchair across the room.

Jo shook her head. 'I'm afraid not,' she had to admit. 'We've only just started. I'm still trying to put together a picture of him in my head.' Jo told him about the visit to his mother's. 'You should have told her to cooperate with the investigation,' she finished, feeling better already for having unloaded her irritation.

Connor ran his hands through his already-tousled hair. 'What can I do? I'm sorry, but did she look to you like the kind of woman you could tell how to behave?' He reached for the gin bottle and topped up Jo's drink and his own. 'She can be difficult, I know.'

Jo felt sympathetic. She had a similar problem with her own mother but she tried not to let this show. 'But she doesn't seem terribly worried about Sean?'

'She subscribes to the school of thought which says if a grown man wants to opt out of his life temporarily then let him.' Connor sighed.

'And you don't?'

'No,' he answered. He downed his drink quickly and set the glass on the high-gloss black table with a definite clunk. 'Not when he owes me money, I don't.'

Jo took a sip of her drink so that she didn't appear to pounce on this information. 'Much money?' she asked, watching her ice cubes bump gently against the lemon.

Connor stood up and wandered towards the window. 'No, not really. Depends on your definition of a high-value sum. I mean everything is comparative—'

'Is that why you want us to find him?' Jo, staring at his broad-shouldered back, recognised this distraction technique and tried to keep Connor on the subject.

'He does pay half the mortgage, which isn't exactly peanuts so I can't fault him there. And, look, I know our family don't exactly come over as all heart but at the end of the day, he is my little brother.' He turned around finally and met Jo's gaze. 'But well — yes — money is part of the reason. I don't want to go into it all now.' He lifted a slat of the blind to look out. 'Tell you what — why don't we eat?' He turned again to smile at Jo. 'Italian? Thai? Indian? What would you prefer?'

It was seriously tempting but Jo reminded herself about her reservations about getting too involved with Connor. She also recalled that he was a Gemini and so could probably talk her into anything after a few glasses of gin. Gathering her things and avoiding his blue eyes, she said she would have to go back to Coventry and should make a start soon. 'There are a couple more things you could help me with, though. Sean had been married, hadn't he? Do you know how we can contact his ex-wife?'

'No point.' Connor poured more gin for both of them, despite what she'd said. 'Valerie left him years ago. I think she's in New Zealand now. She got a job with a travel firm and ended up there.'

'Why did he get divorced?'

'Oh, I don't know. These things happen.' Connor shrugged. Jo picked up her glass again, already feeling a little light-headed, but she slowly took another sip and waited. Geminis can't bear long silences.

Connor fiddled with the cord on the blinds and paced back to the centre of the room. 'What do you want to know this ancient history for? Sean's divorce was eight years ago or more.' He looked at Jo and laughed suddenly. 'Well, I can see you're not going to give up. Sean and Valerie were not married all that long — about two years. He gave her a very bad time, apparently. That was one of the reasons the family fell out with him. I was working away at the time so I never really found out about it.'

'And she's living abroad now?' Jo weighed this up for a moment. 'Could I have a look at Sean's room?'

'Sure.' Connor led the way, still carrying his glass. 'I've accessed his laptop and been through some papers and stuff he left behind. I couldn't find anything to tell me where he was going — except that one bank statement that mentioned the cash withdrawal in Coventry. I can't get into his actual bank account to see if there has been any more action since.'

Sean's bedroom was at the front of the house and he had a desk in the bay window. The room was not as tidy as the one downstairs but it was more comfortable, as Jo expected, knowing Sean was a Taurean. A squashy old armchair took up one corner with speakers placed close by. There was a jumper on the bed, papers on the desk and coins, books and pens on the bedside table. The books in the room were all financial reference books or textbooks. Jo slid back the doors of the wardrobe, while Connor watched silently. Hanging up were suits, jackets, shirts, belts, ties — corporate wear and not much else. There were two suitcases and an empty holdall stacked neatly at the back. The white chest of drawers was also full of clothes. It was not the room of someone who had made a planned departure.

'All his belongings are here, then?' Jo asked, looking around. There was one picture on the wall, a rather soulless black and white photograph of clouds.

'As far as I can tell.'

Jo moved over to the desk. 'Do you mind if I look?'

'Go ahead.' Connor followed her to the window and stood looking out at the street. There were blinds in this room too but he could see out without adjusting them. Jo leaned over the desk, where it looked like Sean had been working on his accounts. There were paper copies showing lists of debits and credits, bank statements, credit card statements for various cards and handwritten sums on scraps of paper.

Jo picked up one of the credit card bills. It seemed Sean spent a lot of money on clothes and petrol. She recognised the name of one garage on the A46 near Coventry, where he had bought fuel on 17 May. So his visit on 18 June might not have been a one-off. She took her notebook out of her handbag and scribbled down the address, although she didn't really think it would get her anywhere.

She cast an eye down the printouts. The details of each transaction were very sketchy and she couldn't deduce much from them. Certainly Sean spent a lot of money but he also had a lot coming in. She picked up a credit card holder lying on the desk and flicked through it. There were one or two loyalty cards for major retailers and some membership cards. One was for a gym in the city, two were for casinos in Knightsbridge and one, which Jo flicked past and then turned back for a closer look, was for a fitness club in Leamington Spa. The club was called Greenaways. She had never heard of the place but Leamington was less than half an hour from Coventry. And it was off the A46.

Jo picked up some more bills. 'Have you looked through all this stuff?'

'Not thoroughly.' Connor was still staring expressionlessly out of the window. 'I had a quick look but all I found were endless bills he's run up in clubs and restaurants, which I knew anyway. You find anything else?'

'No, that's about all there is.' She slipped the Greenaways card into her pocket. She didn't know why she didn't want Connor to know everything just yet but she trusted her instinct. She noted down the names of the casinos to pass on to Alan or Macy.

'Have you finished in here now?' Connor asked. 'I mean, you can take as long as you want but if you're going to take for ever, we may as well go and eat. Believe me, I've had a good look round. These are mainly just papers from the bank. He used to bring a lot of work home.'

They went downstairs. 'Was he doing very well in his career?' Jo asked.

'Not as well as he should have been—' Somewhere in the house a phone started ringing and Connor stopped speaking. He hesitated with one hand on the bannister. 'I'm not going to answer it,' he said. Looking up at Jo and laughing over the ringing sound, he added, 'I mean, no one important is going to call me at this hour. So there's no need.'

The phone had stopped ringing by the time they reached the hall but Connor stood in the hallway, glancing from one room to another as if unsure what to do next. She refused his offer of another drink but she thought he looked like he needed one and said so.

'I'm just not used to living on my own.' He grinned and shook his head at her, as if having a little laugh at himself. 'I admit I do get a bit jumpy.'

* * *

Connor had been unmistakably on edge but perhaps that was reasonable since his brother had gone missing, Jo reflected, as she walked to the Tube station still pleasantly heady from the gin and tonic. It was a warm humid evening, with plenty of people about and even the late commuters seemed to be in their summer clothes. Jo was feeling very satisfied with her day's work. Her earlier grumpiness had faded away, almost certainly assisted by the gin and she was also pleased with herself for not succumbing to the temptation of a meal with Connor. *That would hardly be professional*, she told herself while waiting for the train.

If a slightly guilty memory arose of one very unprofessional but extremely pleasant night with her boss Macy last winter, she pushed it to the back of her mind. *Keep to the case in hand*, she said to herself, as her train pulled in. And during the journey, she did her best to focus on the day's findings. By far the most interesting revelation, she felt, was that Sean owed his elder brother money. Maybe they were both in debt and that was why Sean had made himself scarce? She wondered why Sean had gone to Coventry on 18 June and whether in fact he was still there. Perhaps with his girlfriend Rosie? But she had not seen anything personal among Sean's papers — no photos or cards and no clue to Rosie's identity or whereabouts. It was only Connor's wild guess that she was the link between Sean and Coventry.

The more definite link was in Jo's handbag. She took out the plastic membership card for the club in Leamington.

Greenaways: Exclusive Fitness. Fine facilities in gracious surroundings.

Jo congratulated herself privately. So what if she had nearly been thrown out by a snobby woman and had spent half the day hanging around waiting for trains? She had her first real lead.

CHAPTER FIVE

Jo had arranged to meet Alan at Macy's early the next morning so that she could tell him what she had found out. She regretted this when her alarm clock went off and wished she had not stayed up until three a.m. working on Sean's chart. She showered, made coffee and munched a bowl of granola, which she considered to be very boring food. She ate it for the same reason she went swimming: because it was good for her. She fed Claudius the cat and left her flat at eight thirty, hurrying down the fire escape to the back of the house, where her car was parked.

At eight forty-five she abandoned all hope of driving to work. All she could get out of the ignition was a disheartening click. There was not even the satisfaction of a revving engine. Jo got out and looked under the bonnet but she had only a slim idea what she was looking at. Turning it off and on again often worked with her laptop but the car remained indifferent. Nothing — except the click. She locked it and began the short walk into the centre of Coventry.

Her mind was busy with various car problems, trying to guess how much they would cost to sort out, so it was not until she was walking down the Burges, the busy, narrow street where the agency was situated over a shoe shop, that she remembered that she and Macy had fallen out. She wondered if he was still sulking as she pushed open the blue door and climbed the steep stairs to the first floor. She really preferred to be on good terms with Macy although they could never seem to maintain it for long.

'Jo! How are you? Did you have a good time in London?' At least Celia seemed pleased to see her as usual.

'I'm fine but the car's sick. Anybody in?' Jo took a seat in one of the old armchairs by Celia's desk.

'Yes, Mr Macy's in his office. I expect he'll be out in a minute to say hello.'

'I doubt it.' Jo accepted a coffee from Celia. 'He's not happy with me at the moment. Do you know if anything has happened on this missing person case? Sean Fitzpatrick.'

'What have you done to upset Mr Macy?' Celia grinned at Jo as she reached for the filing cabinet drawer, bracelets jangling. She located the chocolate biscuits and handed the packet to Jo.

'The other day when I was mooching about in his room, he came in and found me. On top of that I had dealt with a client, which led to us getting this Fitzpatrick case,' Jo explained.

'Unforgivable.' Celia shook her head in mock disapproval. 'Now, Fitzpatrick . . .' She scrolled down her screen and read from some notes. 'Mr Macy informed the police on Wednesday afternoon but they weren't able to help. Alan has yet to report—'

She was interrupted by Macy appearing from his office. He stood leaning his long body against the door frame, taking in the scene, eyebrows raised in mild interest. His hair and eyes were the same muddy brown and even when he wore a suit and tie like today, his clothes tended to look crumpled and untucked. Despite this, he still managed to be attractive. Jo tried to ignore it but she knew he felt the same about her. After they had made love that one time on a rainy evening in front of the gas fire in her flat, she knew she should have felt closer to him but she found it easier to revert to their friendly — if uneasy — business relationship.

Macy eased himself into the room in a leisurely fashion. He snaffled a biscuit and looked at her expectantly. 'Got us any more business lately? Anyone bumped into you in the street and begged you to find their long-lost cousin? Or—'

'Sarcasm — the refuge of the desperate man,' Jo asserted, smiling triumphantly.

Macy shot her an exasperated look. 'The question is, is it worth my paying your expenses to London? Alan told me he'd asked you to go.' He pushed open the door of his office and Jo followed him in, aware that Celia was grinning with satisfaction.

Jo described her meetings with Mrs Fitzpatrick and her elder son and her visit to the National Commercial Bank. 'But you don't have to pay me,' she finished, 'Alan and I did a deal.'

Macy didn't argue or ask for explanations. He wrote down the names of casinos Sean visited and said he would check them out.

'I found those in Sean's bedroom,' Jo went on. 'I had a peek when I called to see Connor. He said that Sean owed him money but he didn't tell me how much.'

'So what have you found out about Sean Fitzpatrick? In ten words.'

'He's tough, clever — very ambitious. People like him but he uses them and he's probably promiscuous too.'

'Did you get that from an ex-girlfriend?' Macy asked with characteristic cynicism.

'No. From his chart,' Jo responded. 'He's Taurus with Sagittarius Rising and the Moon in Aries.'

She predicted that Macy was going to make some flippant comment but he was interrupted by the phone. He held the mute button. 'Police,' he said to Jo before engaging with the call.

She was not particularly curious. PI work necessarily overlapped with police work from time to time and she knew Macy had some good contacts in the Coventry station. She only half-listened. Privately, she felt a moment of satisfaction that she and Macy were back on their usual terms.

‘A man’s body,’ she heard Macy say. ‘What, a *dead* body?’ he repeated, somewhat needlessly, she thought. She looked up but he was listening and nodding, which didn’t tell her anything.

‘Do you want to see a corpse?’ he asked as soon as he put the phone down.

‘It wouldn’t be my first choice of entertainment,’ Jo said.

Macy, moving quickly for him, picked up his car keys and headed out of his office. ‘The police have found a body in Gollins Wood, do you know it?’ he called over his shoulder, Jo on his heels. Celia stared after them, indignant that anyone should pass her desk without speaking to her.

‘Yes, it’s near Princethorpe — not far,’ Jo answered. She had to follow him down the dingy corridor at the back of the building to find out more.

‘They called me because they knew we were looking for Fitzpatrick and apparently this could be him.’ Macy led the way through the back door of the office to the narrow alley where his car was parked. ‘They think we might be able to help identify it.’

‘Alan will be mad at missing this.’ Jo fastened her seat belt and Macy manoeuvred the old Ford out of an impossibly small space.

‘Damn. I should have told Celia to let him know where he could find us.’ Macy stopped the car halfway through the ten-point turn and ran back to the office. When he came back he was carrying Fitzpatrick’s file. He dropped it on Jo’s lap. ‘This might come in handy too. See if you can dig out his photograph.’

Jo looked through the thin folder. ‘Did they say what had happened to this body?’

‘They said some kids found it half-buried in the woods.’

‘I don’t see why it should be Sean.’ Jo looked at his photograph: the now oddly familiar square jaw, rugby shoulders, mousy hair and nondescript eyes. Not a handsome face, nor a complicated one, she thought, although his birth chart said otherwise. Jo mentally prepared herself as they drove out of the city. She had seen a dead body only once before. She had managed to forget the details but remembered the experience and was glad she had only eaten granola that morning.

Macy drove to Princethorpe, a sizeable village east of the city, and then demanded directions. Jo directed him through the village and down an unsignposted narrow lane. Macy didn't argue. Jo was a local and he wasn't. She had lived in Coventry all her life until she had left to go to university and it had not changed much in the seven years since then. She knew Princethorpe as a place with a good pub and plenty of walks, which in her experience usually ended up at the said pub. But the wood was quite a long way from the village, near the reservoir, if she remembered correctly. The surrounding area was largely agricultural but some of the woods and hedgerows were still intact and their branches battered the car on both sides as Macy tore along the lanes. On Jo's instructions he turned right on to a B road, which was wider and busier, and then right again.

'This is it,' Macy murmured when the first police car came in sight, parked with two wheels on the grass verge. He pulled in behind it and he and Jo walked in silence up the lane.

Jo could see the garish yellow of rape flowers through the hedge on one side of them. Their sickly oily smell seemed to stick in her chest. On their right was Gollins Wood. Jo had remembered it as a small, pretty, mixed wood. Today it seemed dense and tall. Ahead of them was commotion. They passed several police cars and heard the hiss of voices on radio before they could distinguish the words.

'Hold on.' A police constable stepped out of a car in front and held up his hand. 'You can't go up there just now.'

'Detective Sergeant Anwar asked me to come,' Macy said. The constable thought about it for a long moment, checked his name on a list, asked for ID and then waved them on as if he was on point duty. Further down the road there were more vehicles, including a van, which was parked with two more police cars in a lay-by. Jo scanned them for a newish red Ford Escort, which was Sean Fitzpatrick's car, but it wasn't there.

This lay-by and the path leading off into the woods seemed to be the hub of all the activity. The people milling around purposefully must either be police or the forensic team, Jo guessed, but as almost all wore white coveralls and masks, it was hard even to discern gender, let alone role. A uniformed PC held them on the periphery of all this activity, just outside the taped-off area, where they waited patiently. Jo felt almost mesmerised by the quietly efficient comings and goings in and out of the dense patch of woodland in front of her, where an ominous white tent was already being erected. She breathed deeply, trying to still the jitters in her stomach.

After a few minutes, Jo noticed a person of slight build in a full hazard suit making a beeline towards them. When she removed her mask, it was clear she was an Asian woman with serious, delicate features. It turned out it was actually Macy she was heading for and she addressed him directly without introductions while she was still some steps away. This turned out to be DS Anwar.

'Thanks for coming so quickly. The body's about fifty metres into the woods. Obviously you can't go in,' she added, although neither Macy nor Jo had made a move towards the woods. 'They'll be bringing it out in a minute,' she went on. 'Shallow grave and it's been chewed about a bit I'm afraid.'

Jo's stomach lurched. She fixed her feet firmly on the trampled grass and locked her eyes on the footpath leading into the woods. A portly man in the regulation white suit tramped along it towards them. The bottoms of his synthetic white trousers and his plastic overshoes were covered in mud.

'John Chapple says blow to the back of the head,' he muttered to DS Anwar. 'Dead some days. Food for the foxes, which are a bloody pest around here. Did you get hold of that PI with the picture of one of the mispers?'

DS Anwar looked up. 'Have you got the photo, David?' she said to Macy. David? Jo tried not to look surprised.

Macy's contacts with the local police must be even better than she had thought.

'Sorry. I couldn't bring a photo. One of my investigators has it,' Macy was saying. 'He will be along in a minute.'

The chubby man raised his eyes to the glorious blue sky. Jo said nothing but folded her arms over the Fitzpatrick file. She guessed Macy did not admit to having a copy of the photograph because he thought they would then be summarily dismissed.

Through the narrow gap between the trees, Jo could see an ordered procession approaching. Two constables led the way carrying large, clear, tagged sacks. Behind them were men carrying a narrow stretcher. It seemed to be heavy and their feet slithered on the mud.

The first thing Jo noticed was that the body was not entirely covered up. Flapping from under the black plastic, she could see the dead man's trousers, ripped at the ankle — or maybe bitten? Part of his leg was visible: a white, hairy, muscular calf mangled and smeared with blood and mud. Jo's arms were tensed like steel around the file. She felt they were holding her up. The wavering, uncertain progress of the horizontal body drew nearer.

When the stretcher was within touching distance, DS Anwar put out a gloved hand and spoke to the man holding the back end of the stretcher. Jo didn't hear what was said but the next moment, a zip at the head end of the corpse was tugged back and she was staring down at the dirty white face, which seemed to hover below her. The lips were pulled back in a frozen grimace and Jo could see the white teeth. The top of the head was a horrible, flattened shape covered by matted hair and dried blood.

Jo was having trouble associating this muddy, torn body with the fresh-faced, stolid man in the photograph, the man she had been looking for all day yesterday. And yet at the same time she was sure it was Sean Fitzpatrick. It was something about the square shape of the jaw.

‘I’m pretty sure it’s him,’ she heard Macy say. If Macy hadn’t spoken, Jo would have. The bag was rezipped by an anonymous gloved hand and she watched the stretcher being lifted into the mortuary van.

It was not that she hadn’t considered that Sean might be dead. In fact that was one of the first things that had occurred to her when she had heard Connor Fitzpatrick’s story. Car crash or suicide, she had thought clinically. But her job had been to delve into Sean’s life. Now, having seen his dead body she found herself thinking of the mundane glimpses she had seen of it: his elegant mother, his comfortably untidy bedroom, his office, where his colleagues were mildly curious about his absence, slightly critical about his reputation with women. They were going on thinking of him as being alive.

She had spent hours analysing his character last night and had put out of her mind the thought that she might be casting a dead person’s chart. Sean’s chart had not endeared him to her. He came over as something of a bully. Mercury in Aries in the Fifth House, together with a Sagittarius Ascendant, confirmed he had likely been a gambler and there were indications that this could easily have become a compulsion. On the plus side, he had been bright, decisive and enterprising — and a good communicator. But a badly afflicted Venus meant his attitude to sex had left something to be desired. He had tended to see others as possessions. Jo had not got as far as progressing the chart to see what the future had in store for Sean. It was a good job she hadn’t bothered, she thought blackly.

She stood still while her brain stumbled through these confused thoughts. Beside her Macy was equally immobile. They were unwilling to look up and acknowledge the other’s presence. It was as if they both felt they could only deal with this by pretending they were alone.

Eventually Sergeant Anwar came back to Macy, thanked him and asked him to contact her when he had the photo, which was obviously meant to be their dismissal. Macy chatted with her for a minute, asking her questions, which she mainly avoided answering until she said, 'Listen, David, don't you forget to keep in touch,' in a tone that was somewhere subtle between warning and warmth. With that, she walked back to the crime scene, checking her phone.

Very gradually, Jo lessened the tension in her arms and legs. A hand fell on her shoulder and a cheerful voice said loudly in her ear, 'It's all happening, isn't it? Have I missed the big event?'

'What the hell are you doing?' Jo swung round to confront Alan's impervious grin. She had known it was him. Only one person could generate such enthusiasm when faced with a possible murder. But she was still angry. 'Don't sneak up on me like that. No, it wasn't that much fun,' she told him.

'And yes you are late,' Macy added. 'You've missed the body. It looked like Fitzpatrick to me.'

'You mean they let you get close up?' Alan looked around him with an alert, wide-eyed expression. 'I thought they would just take the photo off you and do the identity bit themselves.'

'I said I didn't have the photo,' Macy sighed.

'Quite right,' Alan said with a nod. 'Gone off to the morgue, has it?' He looked on the ground curiously, as if he half-hoped to see the body lying around. At least Alan, with his usual lack of sensitivity, had jolted them out of inactivity.

Macy started back towards the car. 'I suppose we may as well try to do something useful for our client. Why don't you two stay around here for a while?' he said. 'The police are going to fetch Connor from London. They need a formal identification. I'd better offer to go and see the body with him.'

'The police won't tell us anything,' Jo sighed. She was thinking, somewhat irrelevantly, that she was not wearing the right footwear for a hike in the woods.

'Well, Fitzpatrick must have come from somewhere. There didn't seem to be a car,' Macy said. 'Are there any houses nearby, or pubs?'

'He could have been murdered miles away and just dumped here,' Jo said. She started to think it through. 'Mind you, someone might have seen the dumping.'

'Don't spend too long on it,' Macy said through his car window, 'and don't worry, I'm not exactly going to have a nice afternoon either.'

'So what happened?' Alan said to Jo as they watched him drive off. When she didn't answer, he added, 'I suppose not everyone's got a strong stomach like me.' It was not an apology but it was said like one and Jo stopped glaring at him as they made their way back to the woods. 'I turned over the usual stones yesterday,' Alan rattled on. 'The Sally Army hadn't heard of him. I couldn't find anything on his car — but the police will find that soon enough. I don't see it here.'

'I don't think they've found it. I heard one of the constables say there were no vehicles in the lay-by when the body was discovered.'

As they drew as close as they could get to the scene of the crime without causing too much attention, Jo noticed some of the police cars were leaving and the area around the lay-by was less hectic. There were no houses or buildings in sight.

'Just behind the woods is the reservoir. Do you know it?' Jo asked. 'I think there's a pub there — a new place. It can't be far away. I'll go there if you like.'

It was not just the easiest option, it was the only option, as Jo saw it. She didn't know of any houses nearby and the pub was the only place she could think of that was in walking distance. Alan was quite happy to linger around the crime scene and agreed to meet her at his car in an hour. Jo watched him stomp off towards Sergeant Anwar. He had left his customary anorak at home because of the hot weather and was wearing a hand-knitted cardigan, socks and sandals. Sometimes she forgot how much she could dislike Alan. And this job.

CHAPTER SIX

Jo couldn't bring herself to cut through Gollins Wood although she guessed it would be quicker. The sun was strong and the tarmac felt hot through her espadrilles, but she still preferred to go along the road. Anyway she didn't mind walking further. It cleared her thoughts.

She passed no buildings, just fields and hedges, and wondered what a Londoner like Sean Fitzpatrick was doing around here — dead or alive. So far, his only definite connection with the area seemed to be the fitness club, Greenaways. And civilised, gracious Royal Leamington Spa seemed miles away, although actually it was nearer than Coventry. She must go to that club and see what she could find out — that is, if Connor still wanted to know, Jo reminded herself.

She turned down the lane signposted to Leamington and a glimpse of the reservoir in a slight dip on her left reassured her that this was the right way. Dozens of bright sails billowed to and fro on the sheen of the water, despite the calm day. A little further on, she saw the pub ahead and started to look forward to a cold bottle of beer.

The Castaway had not been open very long, maybe five years. It was the kind of place you drove out to for Sunday lunch in the summer. Jo remembered sitting outside looking at the lake. Had she brought her mother here for lunch one Mother's Day? Yes, that was it. Her mother had said she couldn't eat anything because it was all Indian food.

There was a large car park in front of the pub, which was almost empty. Jo guessed it was early for lunchtime customers. Inside, the smell of last night's beer mingled with frying onions from the kitchens and music was playing very faintly. A man behind the bar was idly stacking tokens for one of the games machines. He looked up when he saw Jo and picked up a tea towel in a business-like manner. 'Hello, what can I get you?'

Jo ordered her cold beer and turned to take in the rest of the place. A huge glass window offered good views of the lake along the back of the room. The décor was light and modern with cane chairs and pastel prints. *Just this side of naff*, Jo thought. Two or three of the window seats were occupied but there was no one else at the bar.

As she paid for her beer, she told the barman she was looking for someone. 'Apparently he comes in here.' Jo handed over Sean's photograph. 'Do you know him?'

The big, moustached man behind the bar looked at it for a second and shook his head. Obviously a man of few words, Jo thought. 'Oh, that's a shame,' she said.

The barman was still holding the photograph. 'Wait there a minute,' he said. 'I'll go and ask the boss.' He took the photograph into the white-tiled kitchen at the back.

The barman came back with a short, unsmiling British Asian man in a crisp blue shirt with the sleeves rolled up. He was looking at the photograph and at Jo. 'Hello. My name is Matti. How do you do. You know this man?'

There was something about his earnestness and air of authority that made Jo decide to lie as little as possible. After all, Sean's death would be big news soon enough. 'Well, I know his brother,' she explained. 'Sean Fitzpatrick — the man in the photo — has gone missing. His brother is trying to find him. I think he may have come in here?'

'Yes, I think so.' Matti stared at the photograph. He placed it on the bar. 'Hold on, I'll get my brother, he does more serving than me.' He left to get reinforcements. The barman looked on, his hands wrapped around his tea towel.

'Sorry I can't help,' he said, when he caught Jo's eye. 'I only work lunchtimes. Never seen him myself. I'm sure of that.' He sounded sorry to be left out.

Matti came out of the kitchens with his brother, obviously younger, in a white kitchen overall. He came up to her eagerly. 'Let me see this photograph. I've a good memory for faces.' Jo handed it over and they all studied it. *This is detection by committee*, she thought. She sipped her beer and waited.

'I've seen him.' Matti's younger brother spoke up. 'Not often. Maybe only once even but he's definitely been in here.'

Jo felt an unexpected rush of satisfaction. 'Can you remember when? How long ago, roughly?'

Matti's brother thought about it while the photograph was passed round again. 'In the last two months, because I've seen him since I came back from my holidays.'

'Shahm went to India in the spring,' Matti explained.

'What about before then?' Jo asked. 'Did you see him before your holiday?'

'I don't think so.' Shahm shook his head. 'But I've definitely seen him since. He was quiet. A whisky drinker, I think, definitely shorts anyway.' He turned to his brother. 'Don't you remember? Someone rang the pub for him and I had to shout his name out — that doesn't often happen.'

'Can't you say for sure when this happened?' Jo asked.

'I really don't know. About a month or so ago, maybe.'

'Was he on his own?'

Shahm frowned, clearly trying to be helpful. 'Sorry. But I do remember he was here. Quite a tall bloke, isn't he? Not very friendly. I think it was early evening because we weren't busy. There was a call for him.' Shahm dipped his head towards the phone behind the bar. 'I called out his name and he came over—'

'Did you say anything to him about the call?' Matti interrupted. 'We don't encourage customers to take calls here. We don't mind if maybe someone forgets their mobile or something like that,' he explained to Jo. 'But we don't like people to make use of the number to just contact people like that.'

Shahm's smooth young face creased up in an effort to remember. 'I don't think I did,' he said. 'I was going to but something stopped me. Maybe I was serving someone else. I think perhaps I didn't want to speak to him because he seemed so bad-tempered.' Shahm avoided Matti's eyes and smiled at Jo. 'Why do you want to know all this?'

'He went missing on the eighteenth of June,' Jo answered. 'The name the caller asked you and you had to shout out — was it Sean Fitzpatrick?'

Shahm looked uncertain. 'Could have been, but I'm really not sure.'

'I don't suppose you remember who rang him? Man? Woman?'

'Woman, I *think*, but . . .' Shahm shrugged. 'Look, I'll keep racking my brain about it. Maybe I'll remember something else.' He looked up at Jo from under long eyelashes. 'Why don't you stay for lunch? I'm cooking today and I'm a good cook—'

'Sorry, I can't, someone's waiting for me,' Jo said. 'But hold on to the photograph.' She handed him a copy. 'One of your customers might recognise him. Let me know if they do.' She gave Shahm her business card and he promised earnestly that he would get in touch if anything else occurred to him.

Behind her a group of men had come in and the barman went off to serve them. They were all young, wearing shorts and had an overtly sporty look. Jo guessed they must be from the sailing club, which was not far away. She asked Matti if she could show them the photograph but they were no use. They giggled together and looked at it blankly. She asked them where the sailing club was and one of them pointed unhelpfully towards the lake.

'I might have guessed it was in that general direction,' Jo remarked. She left by the door in the plate-glass frontage.

It was very warm outside. Jo looked at Draycote Water, hazed and flat below. Really she ought to be starting back to meet Alan but she thought she would try to find the sailing club as it seemed to be the only other place where Sean could have been either going to or coming from. A sign on a wooden fence reminded her she was on land owned by the water authority but a gate stood open and a gravelled path took her to the lakeside.

Despite all the boats on the water, there was nobody about. The reservoir was surrounded by marshy ground with a high concrete dam at one end. She found the clubhouse easily enough, a low structure that looked like it might fall down in a high wind. It had a bar upstairs that could be hired for birthday parties and other functions, if the posters were to be believed, but the building had a temporary look about it.

Jo wandered around to the boathouses where the dinghies were kept. She saw locked sheds with boats, windsurfing boards and mountain bikes inside but there was nobody about to speak to. If Connor wanted them to carry on with the case, she would have to come back for a more thorough look but now she really had to go and meet Alan.

Jo retraced her steps back up to the road. She was puzzled that Sean had been at the Castaway. Apart from the Indian food and the nearby sailing club, it was nothing special. It was nowhere near any large settlement and it was not on a main road. Sean would have had to go out of his way to find it. And why would he have done that?

When Jo reached the road, Alan's ancient estate was waiting for her. He had driven to meet her and when she got in she saw immediately that he was in a self-congratulatory mood. With his old-fashioned side-parting and his square glasses, he reminded her of a game show host fallen on hard times.

'We're a step ahead of the police, anyway,' he announced as he drove off. 'They wouldn't tell me a thing. Just that the bloke had been dead for over a week, which you'd already told me. So I went up the lane and started asking around.'

‘I’m surprised there was anyone to ask,’ Jo said when she could get a word in.

‘There’s a couple of houses and a farm towards Princethorpe. I’ve got a print of Fitzpatrick’s picture so I waved it under the noses of the locals.’

‘And?’ Jo knew there was some news coming and her patience with Alan was wearing thin.

‘No one had seen or heard of him. But—’ Alan paused to heighten the suspense — ‘I had a long talk with the farmer. I told him what had happened and whereabouts. He said two weeks ago he saw a girl and a car in that lay-by. She was having some trouble with the car and she was there quite a while fixing it.’

He seemed to have come to an end. Jo sighed. ‘Is that it?’

‘Well, yes. But he gave a very good description. It was an old blue Vauxhall Astra — 09 registration and a sunroof.’

‘What about the woman?’

‘Hmm? Oh, he didn’t remember her so well. Just said she was tall and blonde and wearing a red-and-white jacket.’

‘When was this?’

‘About quarter to nine, he reckons, because he had just packed up for the day and was driving the tractor back across one of the fields about half a mile from the woods.’

‘If it really was two weeks ago that would be handy because it’s exactly two weeks today since Sean went missing.’

‘That’s right,’ Alan said. ‘Coincidence or what?’ He seemed most pleased to have found out this information before the police. ‘Just as I was coming away, two uniforms were going to the farm,’ he chortled. ‘I bet they hadn’t been to the pub either. By the way, did you get anything there?’

‘Yes, the barman — well, barboy, really — recognised Sean’s photograph and says he was there one night — but he couldn’t remember exactly how long ago. Maybe two weeks or maybe more—’

Alan was longing to interrupt so he could begin an enthusiastic hypothesis but Jo stopped him. ‘Listen, there’s more. Sean received a phone call at the pub. The barman thinks it might have been a woman.'

'Right. I get it. Maybe Sean goes to the Castaway to meet the girl—'

'Yes, but why meet there? Why that pub?'

Alan clearly didn't think this was worth dwelling on. 'God knows,' he said. 'What if he went there two weeks ago today to meet his girlfriend? Say she was the girl the farmer saw in the lay-by and she didn't turn up because her car had broken down.' Alan was getting so enthused about his theory his driving was suffering and he had to slam the brakes on at a red light. 'The girl gives Sean a ring to tell him and—'

'Why not just call him on his mobile?' Jo tried to interrupt but Alan had built up a head of steam and a mere Virgo was not going to stop an Arian in full flow. Jo bided her time, watching the lights change and enjoying a moment of relief that she had managed not to throw up at the crime scene. All she had to do was to survive Alan's driving now.

'Then the poor bloke goes out to help her and gets a bang on the head for his trouble,' Alan went on. 'It's his missus who bumped him off. Must have been.'

'You're making it up as you go along,' Jo said. 'We don't even know if this woman that the farmer saw had anything to do with Sean. Although,' she added, 'Connor Fitzpatrick told me his brother had a new girlfriend called Rosie. But we have no idea if she's a local.'

'We'll have to trace her. Did you find out anything else in London yesterday?'

'Nothing spectacular. Sean's office think he's off sick. His mother didn't seem to care where he was.'

'This Rosie didn't crop up in any of the conversations, did she?' Alan asked. Jo shook her head but he went on undaunted. 'Still, at least I've got a bit of a description plus the broken down car. I'll concentrate on tracing that. The bobbies will turn up Sean's car in no time. Might as well let them do the work for us, as Macy always says.'

He pulled into the car park near Macy's office. Even Jo, who herself had a long stride and walked fast, had trouble keeping up with his energetic pace. They stopped on the way, at her suggestion, for sandwiches. The peanut butter and banana ones she had bought yesterday in London had been substandard but there was a deli in the city centre that made them just the way Jo liked.

Celia said she expected Macy back any minute so Jo ate her sandwiches while Alan regaled them with his theory. Celia was impressed but Macy, when he arrived, was distinctly less enamoured of it. 'Absolute speculation,' he commented when Alan presented the open and shut case.

Alan was not put off his stride. 'You have to admit this Rosie woman is Suspect Number One,' he insisted.

'Do you have to speak in capital letters?' Macy sighed. 'Can't you see I've had a gruelling experience? I've just spent half the day in the mortuary.'

Jo decided to throw her support behind Alan's theory just to be perverse. 'But we're fairly sure Sean was at the Castaway and that he took a call. It's a reasonable assumption that he then went off to meet her in the lay-by.'

'Damsel in distress and all that,' Alan added. 'And he gets a bop on the head for his troubles—'

'Hold on, before you start writing the whole screenplay. Thanks.' Macy accepted coffee from Celia. He was half-lying in an armchair, and as he had most of his staff gathered round him, he was making the most of the dramatic possibilities. 'Point one — we don't know if this Rosie has anything to do with Coventry. Point two — the girl in the lay-by might not have been connected with Sean and, incidentally, I'm not sure a woman would have had sufficient strength to wallop him over the head. He was a big bloke—'

'She might have had help. Anyway, I thought we didn't have to know things for sure. We can deduce,' Jo pointed out. 'I thought that was what detectives were meant to do.'

'We're not detectives, we're investigators,' Macy said. He sipped his coffee. 'As I was saying, point three — we don't even know if Sean Fitzpatrick died anywhere near Gollins Wood. His body could have been dumped there.'

'So why don't you tell us what you've discovered?' Jo demanded. 'While Alan and I have been tramping the dusty lanes of Warwickshire.'

'Oh don't, I'm traumatised,' Macy said. 'I've spent the morning in the mortuary and I'm no good at comforting people.'

'Did Connor take it badly, then?' Jo still felt suspicious of Connor but would have been hard pressed to explain why so she kept this to herself.

'Pretty badly. The police had called him so he was on his way from London when I got to the station. I went with him to see the body and he identified it as his brother. He's still with the police now as far as I know. I've offered to drive him back when they let him go.'

'So he still wants us to keep the case?' Alan asked.

'Yes, that's the only bit of good news I've had all day.' Macy stared into his coffee mug. 'I rang Sergeant Anwar, by the way, and she had some information that might just support your flimsy theory. Apparently Sean had not been robbed. He didn't have much cash on him but he still had all his bank cards, so it was probably him who made that cash withdrawal on the eighteenth.'

'And spent it by the time he died by the sound of it,' Jo pointed out. 'It was for two hundred pounds, wasn't it? Anyway, I think it's important that we find Rosie if that's who the girl in the lay-by is.'

'I'll put out some feelers about the car. I've got a few contacts in that department,' Alan put in. 'Which reminds me. About your car—' He turned to Jo but Macy interrupted with a long-suffering sigh that signalled his defeat.

'All right,' he said. 'Follow up these leads, but we also need to look more closely at Fitzpatrick himself.'

'Sean or Connor?' Jo asked.

'Both, actually, but you've got a good opportunity to find out more about Sean. You've got a second interview at his bank. They rang here this morning. Apparently you applied for a job? Well, you've been shortlisted. I said you would be there on Monday at ten o'clock.'

Jo accepted this calmly. An expenses-paid trip to London was not to be turned down out of hand although she failed to see what more she could find out from the bank. It would be more useful to look for Rosie, but the only possible lead in that direction was the blue Vauxhall and this was very much Alan's department. As he was going to follow that up and Macy was looking after Connor, she found herself superfluous once again.

'When do you want me to look at your car, Jo?' Alan asked, getting to his feet.

'As soon as you can. It's got worse. It's making a terminal clicking noise now and that's all I can get out of it,' Jo explained.

'Sounds like you've bought a pig in a poke to me.'

'Thank you, but it's your advice on the mechanics I'm after, not on my financial decisions.' She shot him a glare.

He took this in his stride. 'All right, I'll come along and look at it now if you like.' That was one of the good things about Arians, Jo reflected. They could dish it out but they could take it too.

During this exchange, Macy seemed to have forgotten they existed and was asking Celia if there was anything around for him to eat. Jo didn't like being ignored, so before she left the office she suggested that Macy ask Connor a couple of questions.

'See if Sean liked sailing or Indian food,' she said in what she hoped was a suitably enigmatic style before she breezed out with Alan in tow.

CHAPTER SEVEN

Watching while Alan delved around in the Renault's engine, Jo realised why Macy put up with him. Rude and bigoted he might be, but he was also reliable and competent. After half an hour or so, he declared the car needed a new starter motor and he could get one now, and at trade price if she wanted.

When he had driven off to get it, Jo went inside, made herself a coffee and mentally reviewed her finances, which never seemed to be healthy. Her recent savings had virtually all disappeared into the car purchase and insurance and she realised she was going to have to put in some more work for Macy now to cover the unexpected expense of the repair.

Of course she would have preferred to rely on her astrology business to bring in the extra money but she was dependent on the orders coming in. She was getting a good following on social media and plenty of interest in her website but the paid work still went in fits and starts. Just before Christmas she had been kept busy doing what really fascinated her: casting charts and progressing them to give an idea of future trends. But this work had dropped off since the spring.

She had a regular income from her weekly horoscope column, which she wrote for a local paper under the name of Giovanna Conti. She had borrowed her paternal grandmother's name thinking it sounded more interesting than Jo Hughes. Even so, her weekly wage didn't quite pay the rent. For the moment, she needed the PI work.

It could be worse. At least working for Macy wasn't boring — and he paid reasonably well. All the same, she must have been mad to think she could afford a car. She wandered out onto the fire escape and looked down at the little white Renault with feelings that were decidedly mixed. Even though she viewed it with distrust for letting her down, she couldn't sell it yet — it would be such an admission of defeat. Thank God Alan's labour was free, anyway, she concluded and went to put the kettle on ready for his return.

Although Alan clearly thought it would be beyond Jo to understand, he did try to explain what he was doing when she asked. To replace the starter motor took him hours of patient work and he eventually overcame his reluctance to ask her for help. It was early evening before they managed to get the engine starting again. When Alan left, Jo just had time to get to the local shop to buy herself some dinner. Out of politeness she had asked Alan to stay but, as she had expected, he hurried home, where she guessed his mother would have his tea warming in the oven.

As she put the key in the door, the phone rang from inside the flat. She hurried towards it, hampered by her carrier bag of shopping, and reached it just before the voicemail message started up.

'Jo! It's Shahm!' came an excited voice down the line. 'You're in at last. You know, from the Castaway. You were here at lunchtime asking about that Fitzpatrick bloke.'

'Oh yes. Hi.' Now that she had identified who was calling, she was unsurprised. Something about Shahm's attentive manner at lunch had told her that having been given her telephone number, he would be likely to use it.

'I've got something for you. Some information.'

Shahm sounded a little hyper, she thought. 'About Sean Fitzpatrick?'

'Yes, but I can't tell you on the phone. I'm at the pub but I can get the evening off. Do you want to come for a drink?'

She didn't really want to go out with Shahm. She had planned to cook herself a meal for a change. She still had some work to do for Macy on checking the would-be nurses' references and she wanted to finish off Sean's chart. 'No, I'm sorry,' she said, 'I haven't eaten all day and I'm going to cook myself dinner and have a quiet night in.'

'Oh . . . I can cook something for you?' Shahm offered.

'That's nice of you, but no — honestly. Look, why can't you tell me this news now? My phone's not bugged, I promise.'

Shahm agreed reluctantly. 'I know now why you were asking questions at lunchtime. About that customer. He's dead, isn't he? The police came round.'

'Yes. It looks like he was murdered and his brother is paying us to find out more about it.'

'I thought a bit more about him and I'm sure I only saw him that once maybe two or three weeks ago. I asked some of the regulars who come in after work most nights. One of them remembered him.'

'Go on.' Jo slid down the wall to sit on the floor beside her shopping.

'He's a guy called Ben — he's about the same age as me and works at the Jag.' Jo recognised the local nickname for the automotive company in Coventry. 'He lives not far away,' Shahm went on. 'He doesn't remember much about the man that died but he tried to chat up the girl he was with.'

'Fitzpatrick was with a woman?' Jo repeated. *That probably puts paid to Alan's theory*, she thought.

'Yes. Ben was chatting to her because she was sitting on her own and the place was virtually empty. This would be around seven, I think. She said her name was Rosie—'

'Definitely Rosie?'

'Yes, a pretty blonde girl with long legs, Ben said.' Shahm paused. 'I prefer dark-haired girls myself.'

Jo laughed. 'Go on. Tell me more about this woman. Do you remember her?'

'No, I don't recall seeing her but I believe him. Why would he make it up? I didn't even tell him that Fitzpatrick had been murdered. I couldn't — the police asked us not to mention it to the customers just yet.'

'What else did he say about her? Does he remember the day?'

'Thinks it was a Friday about two or three weeks ago. He remembers this Rosie was quite friendly at first, said she was an actress. She said she was waiting for someone and Ben shouldn't hang around — that bit might have been just to get rid of him. But she was telling the truth because Ben remembers seeing her sitting with a guy later.' Shahm came to a halt. 'That's about it, really. Can you tell us anything about how this Fitzpatrick was killed? Did you see the body? Was it, like, really gory?'

'It was pretty horrible. It had been eaten by foxes and God knows what,' Jo told him, guessing this would go down well.

'I didn't know you got female private detectives,' Shahm confided. 'I didn't even know you got actual private detectives at all, to be honest.'

They chatted for a while about the strange nature of her job and Shahm said he wanted to cook her a lamb korma, which was his speciality. Jo promised to call in at the Castaway sometime. She had no idea that when she did, she would be in no mood to enjoy Shahm's cooking.

CHAPTER EIGHT

Somewhat to Jo's surprise, the next morning the car started first time. She had been intending to walk into Coventry but she couldn't resist trying it out. Pleased with life — even pleased with Alan — Jo sat there for a few minutes grinning like an idiot and listening to the engine ticking away. As it was working, she decided she might as well drive it into town — although she knew that taking a car into Coventry on a Saturday morning was not good for the environment nor her patience. She ignored these thoughts, pulled the car into first gear and drove off, feeling decidedly cheerful.

Jo was not what you might call a patient driver. In common with many Virgos, her normally temperate and reasonable nature seemed to undergo a transformation when she was behind a steering wheel. It was simply that when concentrating on driving, she forgot to conceal her innate belief that everyone apart from herself was totally incompetent, which she usually disguised very successfully. Finding herself behind a lorry festooned with bunting, slowly making its way to join the rest of the carnival procession, her good mood evaporated in seconds. She overtook it rashly on the only bend in the Kenilworth Road, provoking an outraged flash of headlights from an innocent Mini coming the other way.

By the time she arrived at the Belgrade Theatre, she felt irritable, grimy and sweaty. She caught sight of her flushed face, glaring back at her from the rear-view mirror. Her hair was already looking disordered. She pushed back some curly strands from her eyes and brought her mind to the subject in hand. If Sean's girlfriend Rosie was an actress, the most obvious place to look for her was the Belgrade, which was the only professional theatre in Coventry.

She read the car parking charges, looked round and couldn't see any traffic wardens so decided to risk not paying. The stage door was locked so she strolled round to the front of the theatre. It was a plain building from the outside but the sparkle of lights through the glass doors gave the hint of a more lavish interior. There was a coffee bar near the entrance, which was doing a good trade and, hearing the sound of fractious babies from nearby, Jo hurried past towards the box office, which was simply a large desk in the foyer. The woman behind it listened to Jo's odd enquiry intently but denied any knowledge of an actress called Rosie.

'There are any number of people who perform here. We don't keep records of them all and even if we did, you don't have any dates. You see, we haven't got a permanent company here,' she added. 'Why do you want to know?'

Jo produced her prepared story. 'She came to a party at my flat and left her coat behind. I thought I should try to find her but all I really know is that she's an actress so I thought she must work at a theatre in Coventry. This is the obvious place to start.'

The woman behind the desk pursed her lips and looked into the distance to indicate she was giving the matter some serious thought. Jo detected an element of distinct scepticism in her eventual response, however. 'There are quite a few amateur theatre companies in the area,' she said, as if she was admitting something distasteful. 'But if your friend said she was an *actress* — or should I rather say *actor* — that does imply that it's her *job*, doesn't it?'

'That's what I thought,' Jo said. 'Any ideas about where else I could try?'

The other woman seemed to shed her suspicions and accept Jo's question as a way to pass the time on a slow morning. 'Well, there's the Arts Centre at the university but they tend to have very short runs — a week at most. When was your party?'

'Two weeks ago. The eighteenth of June, actually.'

'You see, if she had been working here then she would have moved on by now. So you'll have to look further afield. In Birmingham there's the Rep, the Hippodrome and the Alex — you'd need to find out what was playing on the eighteenth to see if she's still around. Look at the websites, you should be able to see the cast lists.'

Behind Jo, a family had arrived to buy some tickets, so she moved aside and thanked the woman for her help.

'You might try the Spa Centre at Leamington,' the woman added before turning to her customers. 'They've got a variety show that's been running all summer. It's not *acting*, of course, but . . .' She followed this up with a look, which finished the sentence.

The day was already warming up and some people were sitting in the square outside the theatre. Kids were leaning over the side of the fountain, threatening to fall in. The woman was right, there were easier ways of searching for Rosie and she didn't fancy having to trek round the many theatres in Birmingham. She would check them out online, Jo thought, making her way back to the car. But the Spa Centre at Leamington wasn't far away and the idea of a jaunt there appealed. At the same time, she could have a look at Greenaways Fitness Club. The membership card was still in her handbag. Macy had shown no interest in it but she was convinced it was worth following up.

She lost her way in Leamington trying a shortcut that worked perfectly well on foot, but she eventually found her way to the Parade, which was crowded with Saturday shoppers. Jo was watching out for the more suicidal ones and almost missed someone turning up one of the wide, shady roads. There was a big space in the row of imposing white houses, like a gap tooth. This was the concrete arena in front of the Spa Centre. Jo sometimes went to see films here.

Parking was easy, but when Jo walked over to the theatre she saw it had a distinctly closed look about it. A 'Summer Special' was advertised, just as the woman in the Belgrade box office had said, but unlike the Belgrade, there seemed to be nowhere to buy tickets for it. She went round the back but the place seemed to be completely closed and there was no one around to ask when it might be open.

Jo had imagined that finding an actress in a relatively small city like Coventry would be easy. Now it seemed she would have to look up which repertory companies had been working in all the local theatres since the middle of June. But she was convinced it was worth pursuing. If this blonde woman had been seen with Sean on the night he died, she must be important, she thought as she returned to her car. Rosie must be Sean's reason for coming to this area. She had yet to come up with any other explanation.

Maybe the Greenaways Club could provide another. As it was only a short distance away, according to the map on her phone, she went on foot and walked past the place by mistake. Greenaways was nothing if not discreet. Retracing her steps, she noticed the brass plaque beside the sober Prussian blue front door. She walked up the steps, which were bounded by a graceful iron balustrade, pushed the bell and waited. She guessed a fitness club would be a smart version of the many private gyms she walked past every day on her way into Coventry but this place looked more like solicitors' or architects' offices.

'Good afternoon,' came a sexless voice through a speaker, and Jo asked if she could come inside.

There was a long pause before she was buzzed in, during which she noticed a camera lens peering through the ivy foliage. This made her even more curious but once inside, the place was innocuous enough. She stepped into a wide lobby with black and white tiles on the floor and six-foot-high palm and fig trees grouped in the corners. At the back of the lobby, two women in identical green tracksuits were talking quietly over a curved wooden desk.

The woman with her back to Jo threw a look over her shoulder. 'I might be back this evening, Jane. I've got some more practice to do. Bye.' She picked up a sports holdall and walked past Jo on the way to the front door. The identical green tracksuits and scraped back blonde ponytails made them look a bit like androids, Jo thought.

Jane, who remained standing behind the desk, turned to her. She was a head taller than Jo with wide athletic shoulders.

'I'm thinking of becoming a member,' Jo said. 'Can you give me any details about the club?'

'I can give you a brochure.' Jane handed over a glossy pamphlet. By her accent she was Australian. 'But I can't do much else because today is a men's day. We have single-sex days twice a week. It makes people feel more relaxed.'

'I'm looking for a club that has very extensive facilities — particularly swimming and weights, that sort of thing,' Jo said to keep the conversation going.

Jane's expression said this was stating the obvious. 'You've seen the website?'

'Oh yes.' This was a blatant lie. She had intended to look up Greenaways online but had somehow not got round to it. 'But it was all very unclear, it didn't give me enough detail.'

Jane was now staring at her without blinking. 'OK.' She stretched the two letters into a virtual sentence. 'Perhaps you could give the club a ring after you've read the brochure. But we do have a long waiting list for membership.'

'That's a shame. I particularly wanted to join this club. It was recommended to me by a friend,' Jo continued, pretending she was the kind of insensitive soul who didn't recognise the end of a conversation when she heard it. 'His name's Sean Fitzpatrick. Do you know him?'

'Not offhand. Is he a member?'

Jo produced the plastic card. 'I think so. He gave me this.'

Jane glanced at it. 'That's only a day ticket, not a full membership card. He must have spent a day here once.'

Jo did not have to call on her acting skills to sound disappointed. 'Oh, I'm sure he told me he was a member. Is there any way you can check?'

'Yes, but there's no need.' Jane's fixed smile was starting to look a little strained. 'I can tell he's not a member from that card.'

'But he's probably got a membership card as well,' Jo said.

The other woman sighed and sat down to tap something into the keyboard in front of her. 'No, he's not on here,' she announced with some satisfaction. 'We don't keep a list of day visitors — only members.'

By leaning over the low desk, Jo could see the computer screen reading *No records found*. 'Thank you anyway,' she said. 'I wonder why he said he was. I'll think about joining myself.' She moved away from the desk and Jane smiled politely. 'By the way,' Jo added as an afterthought, 'you don't know anyone called Rosie, do you?'

Jane looked bemused. 'Yes, I know a few girls called Rosie and one puppy, but what does that have to do with the price of bacon?'

Jo grinned. 'Another friend. A friend of Sean's too, as a matter of fact. I don't know her surname—'

'Well, I'm not searching our records for all the Rosies and I wouldn't be allowed to give you any information anyway.' Jane shifted her gaze around the reception area as if hoping for rescue from this tenacious madwoman. When nothing came and Jo remained standing there, she added in exasperation. 'Look, did this Rosie say she was a member too? Because if it's any help, I can't recall any members with that name so I think your friends may be telling you porkies. The only Rosie I know actually works here and she wouldn't go around telling people she's a member—'

'A Rosie who works here?' Jo took a step forward again. 'Is she here now?'

'No. She's only part-time. Look, what is this all about? What do you want with Rosie?'

'Well, I suddenly remembered Sean said a girl called Rosie recommended this place to him. I just wondered if she was around—'

'She's just left. In fact, she passed you on the way out.'

Jo looked round as if the woman with the holdall would magically reappear. She could only recall that she was tall and fair. 'When will she be back?'

'Maybe tonight. She uses the studio on the top floor to practise in. She's a dancer. Just works here mornings — but not tomorrow,' Jane added. 'She doesn't work Sundays. And there is really nothing more I can tell you.' Jane ended on such a note of finality that Jo suspected she may call for help to evict her if she outstayed her welcome any longer.

'Thanks. I might pop in and see her some time,' Jo said with a smile and left the club with mixed feelings. It was impossible to know if Rosie the dancer was the same as Rosie the actress who had been in the Castaway and she doubted if she would be able to call back at Greenaways later to find out because she had promised to meet her sister. Her elder sister Marie was not one to tolerate flaky arrangements, partly because she had to have her own life organised like a project plan. Jo gazed at the clock in the car and sighed. She decided she would just have to tell Macy and if he thought it was important enough, no doubt he would send Alan. She seemed to be doing all the legwork and missing all the fun with this case so far anyway.

Before she set off, she glanced through the brochure, which boasted about excellent sports facilities and an exorbitant membership fee. She stuffed it into her glove compartment, which she had already filled with any maps and guidebooks she could find, and decided to drive to see her sister. As Marie had not seen the car, Jo felt it was her sisterly duty to go and show it off.

Marie was married with two small sons, who made a gratifying audience. Jo's nephews asked to be taken for a ride so she took them to see the ducks in the park. Afterwards, tired out by their current craze for piggybacks, Jo was easily persuaded to stay for dinner. Marie's cooking was not lightly refused. But it meant that by the time she drove back to the centre of Leamington it was nine o'clock and beginning to get dark. Instead of driving straight back to her flat, she couldn't resist going past Greenaways again.

CHAPTER NINE

At this time in the night Jo could park outside the club. She sat in her car and looked up at the Georgian, double-fronted facade. Downstairs the windows were long and elegant, their height decreasing with each floor. The white stucco was flawless, the hanging baskets dripped foliage onto the painted wrought iron around the stairs and basement. The place was prosperous and well looked after.

She noticed some lights in the small square windows on the top floor. Hadn't Jane said the dance studio was up there? Jo wondered if Rosie had come back to practise, as she had said she would. She tried the front doorbell but there was no answer. She took out Sean Fitzpatrick's membership card and swiped it across the slot below the microphone but, unsurprisingly, the door didn't open.

She descended the steps and gazed up at the building again. There were no cars outside, so if Rosie or anyone else was in there, where had they parked? Perhaps there was another entrance round the back. She turned the corner and walked along a little way. She knew these Regency houses usually had rear access. Sure enough, there was a dimly lit, wide, stone-flagged alley running behind the row of houses.

The alleyway was sufficiently dark to cause Jo to hesitate at the corner. Her lips felt dry and her pulse had picked up.

She reminded herself that she was in one of the most respectable parts of town and she may just find out a little more. With this firmly at the front of her mind, she pressed on along the worn flagstones. The subtle scent of privet reaching her from the walled gardens seemed to reinforce her reassurance to herself that, really, she couldn't be anywhere safer.

Greenaways was the third building along. It had large wooden doors wide enough to get a car through. She tried one of them. It opened, and she stepped into a paved yard. A single tree threw darkness in one corner. Across the yard were bins and basement steps and above that, French windows leading onto a veranda. There was no sign of what went on inside or of any life until Jo heard the quick patter of footsteps from the side of the house.

It took one frozen second for her to realise what the sound actually was. Then it appeared. Waist-high, black and running. It didn't bark and she could hear its claws on the cobbles and the jingle of its collar. She could see its teeth as it ran at her.

From somewhere in the depths of her mind she dragged up advice on confronting dogs. *Don't run*, she said to herself. Her feet felt immovable anyway. She knew she should have shouted as well but couldn't summon any sound.

The dog came within snapping distance and stopped, growling. It had a blunt head and wet yellow teeth. It shifted its weight and rolled its head as if it wanted to come at her but was restrained by an invisible leash.

Jo's neck was rigid with fear. Her muscles had turned to chains rooting her to the spot. The dog barked. The blast of sound and hot breath terrified her.

She leaped back. Its head was near her armpit. She smelled the animal's hot breath. It barked again, bellowing deep and loud, and bounded forward. She backed away, fast, stumbling.

The dog's teeth clamped around her sleeve. She kept moving back, her eyes on the gate, at the same time trying to struggle out of her jacket. A force like a truncheon blow struck her on her arm and shoulder and she went down. Her face hit blue paving with the barking ringing loud in her ears. The dog was standing on her back.

There was a shout. Loud, harsh and unmistakably authoritative. Instantly the dog stiffened and hesitated. Jo lay very still, the ground cold and gritty beneath her.

The shout came again and the dog's weight moved off her. Jo couldn't understand what the person was shouting and didn't care. It had worked. Above her there was scuffling, scraping of claws on paving, subdued growling and muttered commands.

'You can get up now.'

Jo realised she had her eyes closed. She opened them. There was the blue paving. She sat up slowly. Her left side felt jarred. She was looking at strappy sandals so white they seemed to glow in the dark, painted toenails and brown shiny legs. The dog was still there but held by the woman, who was wearing shorts and looking down at her with a mixture of wariness and disgust. Jo still didn't care. She mainly felt grateful. She could feel herself shaking and couldn't seem to say anything.

'Who in God's name are you?' The woman had a strong northern accent and a round doll-like face, framed with pale wavy hair. 'What are you doing in the yard?'

'I couldn't get in the front way,' Jo managed. It was beyond her ingenuity just then to make up a story but she began working on one as she got gingerly to her feet, her eyes on the dog. It growled louder but the woman had her fingers in its collar and the other hand holding a chain lead.

'I'm not surprised,' the woman said. 'We don't let just anybody in.'

Jo saw them in perspective now. The dog was a Dobermann, brown and black with massive paws, and its head came up to the woman's elbow. She was small and neat and frowning. Jewellery glittered on her fingers and throat.

Jo hunted up a good reason for trespassing. 'I was meeting Rosie. She said to come round the back if the front door was locked.' Examining herself for damage, she noticed that her expensive denim jacket was torn and wondered if she could sue.

'Rosie left half an hour ago,' the other woman said. 'I'll have to have a word with her about arranging to meet friends here. It's not on.' She stared at Jo in obvious annoyance before she added, 'I'm sorry about the dog, but Rupert was only doing his job. I suppose you'd better come in for a minute if you've hurt yourself.'

Jo looked down at her knee and saw blood. Until then she had only been aware of a stinging sensation but suddenly it hurt and her face felt sore too.

'I'll put Rupert away and clean that up for you.' The smaller woman led the dog, still held close, back up the yard and Jo followed slowly behind. It was somehow irritating to have been attacked by a dog called Rupert. She decided that when she recounted this incident to Macy the dog would have to be renamed Mugger, Slugger or Bugger. She stopped a hysterical giggle before it could get a hold and watched with some satisfaction as Rupert was shunted unceremoniously into a small modern conservatory. Once shut in, he went and lay down on a mat.

Jo felt her breath coming more easily now there was glass between her and the dog. But it still took a bit of courage to walk past it to where the woman was holding the back door open. Jo went through into a kitchen which was almost as spruce and clean-looking as the woman herself.

'Sit down and I'll get you some tea,' she ordered. Jo sat by a white marble breakfast bar while the woman briskly filled the kettle and set out two mugs. Jo couldn't imagine anything as untidy as cooking going on in such a kitchen.

A first aid box was produced and the woman sorted through it. Her tanned hands were deft, her movements quick and practical, her lips pursed. She reminded Jo of a nurse but her perfume was too strong and her lip gloss too shiny. Jo watched as she mixed antiseptic with warm water.

'That was a bit stupid, trying to get in round the back, you know. But Rosie knows about the dog. She's a very silly girl, telling you to meet her there. And then not waiting for you.'

Jo felt a pang of guilt as her story had clearly landed Rosie in it. Still, Rosie only had to deny all knowledge of her and all, presumably, would be well. She wondered what would happen if this woman ever looked at the CCTV of today's visitors, in which Jo no doubt featured. There was no use worrying about that now though.

'Actually I'm interested in joining the club. Do you run it?' Jo asked. She accepted a mug of strong sugared tea, which she normally would have poured away.

'Yes. I'm Kelly Greenaway.' The doll-faced woman smiled suddenly. Jo put down her mug to shake the small hand. 'If you really want to join, I'll just do your knee and then I'll show you round if you like.' She bent down to examine the cut. 'Almost everyone's gone home now but me, I virtually live here — as my husband is always saying — so another few minutes won't make any difference.' She swabbed Jo's knee with cotton wool soaked in the antiseptic solution.

'Thank you. That would be nice,' Jo said faintly. The cut was not a dog bite, as she had first thought, but a bad graze where she had fallen. Other injuries amounted to a very sore left side and what felt like a cut on her face.

'I feel bad that a member of my staff was so irresponsible. Mind you, it's typical of Rosie to forget about the dog and the arrangement. She's wrapped up in herself.' Kelly's ministrations were brief and to the point and Jo was feeling better by the time she had finished the tea.

'If you leave your jacket here, I'll have it mended,' Kelly said with a wave of her hand. 'There's a wonderful old-fashioned tailor in town who does all sorts of alterations. Being short, I'm always going there to have my dresses and trousers taken up.' Kelly smiled again and the atmosphere between the two women became a degree warmer.

Jo agreed to leave the jacket although she thought Kelly was being overgenerous. If she tried to sew it herself, she knew it would never look wearable. Feeling that she might as well find out everything she could about the place now that she had been to all this trouble, Jo asked Kelly if she really would show her round. 'Rosie told me how you've got all the best cutting-edge equipment,' she added, trying to redress the balance for Rosie a little and save the unknown woman from a bollocking.

'Of course, if your knee's not too stiff for a walk. I'd put a plaster on it but I think a graze like that is best left to the air.'

'I'm fine,' Jo assured her and it wasn't until she slid off the stool that she felt how painful her shoulder was. She touched it experimentally as she followed Kelly out of the kitchen.

'I love showing people round.' Kelly steered Jo towards a door on one side of a wide corridor. 'I don't often get the chance. I'm usually in the office. We'll start with the gym.'

She opened the door to a high-ceilinged room, which would probably have been the sitting room of the house when it was built. She flicked on lights which were bright enough to grace an operating theatre to reveal a white-painted gym with mirrors down one wall and the long windows opposite. The gym wasn't large, with only about twenty pieces of equipment in the room. Jo could recognise a cross trainer and a treadmill but most of them looked completely alien.

'This is one of our two high-energy rooms,' Kelly Greenaway announced. 'The equipment is the most sophisticated you will find. Each piece will pair with your phone and recognise you, what settings you need and where you are up to in your activity journey. Are you interested in any form of exercise in particular?'

'No — not yet anyway,' Jo said. 'I swim regularly.'

Kelly nodded enthusiastically. 'Absolutely the best thing for you.' They crossed the dim, echoing foyer with its oval reception desk. The room on the opposite side was almost identical except it contained mainly weight training equipment. Jo thought that if the place hadn't looked so clean, it could have passed for a medieval torture chamber.

'I'll show you the pool next, then. We've got a sauna, plunge pool and a hot spa as well as a tepidarium down there. You look in reasonable shape, to be honest.' Kelly threw a long backward glance at Jo as they went down some stairs. 'Do you just want to tone up or do you have a particular fitness goal?'

The pool was about a quarter of the size of the public one she was used to in Coventry but it looked invitingly tranquil. 'Yes. Well, I do a sedentary job so I don't get much exercise.' Jo's voice bounced off the tiles.

'What is it you do?' Kelly asked. She walked around the pool to tidy up some flotation aids that were lying around. Jo wondered if it was a strain to run a place like this and have to be a walking advertisement. Kelly's upper arms alone clearly showed how much she worked out. Jo reckoned the woman was in her early thirties, which would make her about five years older than herself, and felt doubtful that she would look that good in five years' time.

Jo decided to tell part of the truth. 'I'm an astrologer.'

Kelly looked up, her immaculate eyebrows raised. 'Really? I'm fascinated with it myself. Do you do consultations? I've had my birth chart done but I'd love someone to explain it to me. It's one of those ones you can send for online and the explanations that came with it were a bit vague. Are they any good?'

'They vary,' Jo explained as they went back upstairs, 'but they all benefit from having a one-to-one with a professional astrologer to help you interpret the chart and answer your questions. I could help you with that.' There were squash and badminton courts for Jo to admire on the first floor along with well-equipped changing rooms, lockers and showers.

'Yes, I would like that,' Kelly said. 'I'm Aquarius and I warn you that everything in my chart will tell you that

I'm too scatty and left-field to be a business woman.' She laughed.

Jo was never very sure about Aquarians. No sooner did she think she had them pinned down, than she met one who bore no relation to the others. One thing was certain, though — Kelly was not the airhead she was presenting herself as. Jo detected a cool, shrewd brain beneath the synthetic exterior.

'It depends on the rest of your chart,' Jo said. 'Anyway, Aquarians can usually manage to be more than one person at a time.'

'That's very true,' Kelly agreed, becoming more animated. 'When I'm at home with Mark I like being chilled out and a bit dippy. It's relaxing. And when I'm here, I become all assertive. I'm different again with Nuala, that's my daughter. I have to be in control then — she's only three. This is our dance studio, by the way.'

Rosie — or whoever had been there last — had left the lights on in the deserted studio and Kelly flicked them off one by one. 'Well, what do you think of the place?'

Jo made appreciative noises as they travelled down in a glass lift. She was impressed, but she knew she could never afford membership. In her pocket she had been holding Sean Fitzpatrick's membership card. She was determined to get him into the conversation somehow. Kelly presented her with the opportunity as she led Jo through the shadowy reception area. 'How did you hear about this place or was it just a chat with Rosie?'

'Actually I heard about it from a friend. Sean Fitzpatrick. Do you know him?'

Kelly was tapping the alarm system near the front door. 'I'll let you out this way.' She paused and seemed to give the question some thought. 'No, I don't know the name . . . Is he a member?'

Jo didn't see the point in getting Kelly to check the computer again. 'I don't think so. But he used to go on about this place. I haven't seen him for a while. Rosie knows him too,' she added with an inspired touch.

'Does she?' Kelly sounded vague and uninterested. They had clearly reached the end of their tour. Jo glanced around the spacious reception area with the brochures stacked neatly on the high desk, blank computer screens just below it and alongside them two live screens showing the blurry images from the CCTV. No one had noticed her earlier entrance, Jo noted. Maybe at the back of the house, Rupert took the place of CCTV.

'Now you will think about joining yourself, won't you? And are you serious about looking at my birth chart?' Kelly said.

'Yes, send it to me and once I've interpreted it, I'll bring it over and we'll go through it.'

Considering they had not had the best start, she had found herself warming to Kelly and she meant it when she thanked her for the tour. She was careful to hand over the card that she used for her astrology work, rather than the business card from Macy and Wilson.

'You can tell me about it when you come and pick up your jacket,' Kelly suggested and this arrangement suited them both.

Jo left Greenaways feeling philosophical. OK, so she hadn't found out any more about Sean Fitzpatrick, and she was no nearer knowing whether the Rosie who worked there was his girlfriend. But she did have some valuable new astrology business and Kelly, who clearly ran the place like clockwork and managed to look immaculate too, might be an interesting subject. Jo wouldn't have minded being a member of her smart club. Maybe after a few more consultations among Kelly's rich friends, she might be able to afford it.

At the moment, all she really wanted to do was to climb into a hot bath and nurse her injuries. This small achievement was easily accomplished but as she stretched her aching side in the warm water there was one niggling little thought. She was sure she had seen Kelly somewhere before.

CHAPTER TEN

Jo had a poor night's sleep. She hadn't exactly had nightmares but she had woken up a few times in the night thinking about the dog attack.

After a coffee in bed, she examined herself in the tall bedroom mirror. Her left side felt worse but her other injuries were only grazes. Going up to the glass, she studied the scratches on her face. Her grey eyes looked pretty much the same as usual — not black and swollen as she had half-feared. She hoped the cuts left by the gravel wouldn't bruise.

Washing the car seemed a good antidote for the vaguely anxious feelings left behind from yesterday. So she walked down to the local shop, which sold sachets of car cleaner that promised to wax at the same time as washing. She found a bucket under the sink, filled it with warm soapy water as directed and carried it carefully down the fire escape using her right arm. She had been brought up to believe that those who had cars washed them on Sundays. She didn't imagine for a moment that washing the car would become a regular weekly habit but she thought she might as well start off the right way.

The car was parked on the tarmac at the back of the old Victorian house. Although it was about ten o'clock by the time she got started, it felt like early morning. None of the other residents were about, the sun was hazy and the birds sang loud and undisturbed in the gardens nearby. She was at the rinsing stage when Macy strolled round the corner.

'How suburban of you,' he commented when he saw her. 'I tried the front door but there was no answer so I thought you might be out here.'

'I can see how you got to be where you are today.' Using her good arm, Jo threw the bucket of water at the car and Macy took a nervous step back. In his jeans and cream shirt, with his sunglasses dangling from the pocket, he looked at his best. Jo took this in, while appearing to concentrate on where exactly to throw the next bucket of clean water.

'How did you hurt your face?' Macy leaned across the bonnet so he could see her properly.

Jo told him as briefly as possible, not wanting to dwell on the subject. Macy didn't say much. He told her the scratch on her face was only noticeable to a trained observer like himself.

'I thought I might get a black eye. How would that go down at my interview at the bank tomorrow?' She gave a laugh at the thought of it. 'I'm sure I'm going to be imagining all dogs are out to get me from now on.'

'Even chihuahuas?' Macy asked. He stepped away from the car and studied it. 'So this is it? I can see I don't have to accuse you of choosing a car to boost your image.'

'I don't have to worry that my choice of car says something about the size of my penis, as men do,' Jo remarked. That was proof she was feeling randy, she thought, because that word had suddenly appeared in her head from nowhere. Her aches couldn't be too bad after all.

'Just as well or your decision-making would have been an even more agonised process.' Macy looked more at ease now the last bucket of water had been despatched. 'Do you want to take me out in it, then? Prove that it goes?'

'All right, come in for a drink while I get changed.' Jo was conscious that the way she looked in her wet and ancient dungarees was far from glamorous. She gave Macy a beer and left him in the deckchair with the Sunday paper while she went to put on a summer dress, which made her feel less like a grubby mechanic.

'Have the police turned up anything yet?' she asked when she rejoined him on the landing of the fire escape.

Macy looked up from the sports page. 'They've got the weapon, a wooden hammer — could be a croquet mallet.'

'Ah, a classy murder. Sorry, go on.'

'It was in the woods not far from the body. According to Anita, they've been trying to trace witnesses—'

'Anita?'

'Sergeant Anwar,' Macy answered. 'She says they haven't got very far with that. Apparently they've found the Astra that the farmer saw parked in the lay-by. It was abandoned in a lane the other side of Princethorpe. It's a bit of an old wreck and might not have anything to do with the case.'

'Who owns it?'

Macy shook his head. 'Anita says they haven't traced them yet but of course, Alan thinks he can do better. He reckons if it was sold in Coventry, he'll know who by and who to in no time.'

'Yes, he would say that, but he also said the police would find Sean's car.'

'No. No news about that.' Macy folded up the paper. 'I've been thinking about Sean Fitzpatrick. We don't know much about him really, do we? What did he do when he wasn't at work? What sort of person was he? Have you any idea?'

After the routine exchange of insults, Macy and Jo had returned to the only other kind of conversation they were relaxed with — work. Jo picked up her car keys and locked the back door of the flat. 'According to his chart, he's the kind of person who didn't have much of a life outside work. Earning money was very important to him.' She led the way down the fire escape. 'He liked a bit of excitement too. I don't think I'd have liked him much — he was too volatile and self-centred. He was bright, there's no doubt about that, but devious. An unusual Taurean.' Her work on Sean's chart was virtually finished and revealed a strong but flawed character. She had written it up as positively as she could to present to Connor but it had not been an easy job. 'Where shall we go?' she asked as she settled behind the wheel.

'A round-the-world trip, judging by the amount of maps you've got,' Macy said, peering into the glove compartment. 'As long as we're prepared to travel at seventy miles an hour, of course.' Jo glared at him. 'What about Stratford? We can feed the ducks with this old sandwich I've just found in here.'

'Oh, yes, I remember that one. I didn't like the bread, it tasted rubbery.'

It was not until they were bowling along the bypass that it occurred to Jo why Stratford was a particularly good place to visit. 'Of course, Stratford! I can carry on looking for Rosie there.' She turned her head to glance at Macy. 'What's at Stratford?' she demanded.

'Ducks,' he suggested.

'What else?'

'Tourists. Expensive restaurants. I don't know.' Macy was rubbish at guessing games. He was really no fun at all, Jo thought.

'Only one of the most famous theatres in the country,' she said.

'I'm not going to one of those long Shakespeare plays,' Macy said. 'I'm only interested in the ducks.'

'No, no.' Jo was patient. 'I've been looking for theatres and I forgot the Royal Shakespeare, which is virtually on our doorstep, and so did the woman at the Belgrade.' She didn't know if Macy was keeping up with this but she carried on anyway. 'You know I've been trying to trace Rosie, who was with Sean in the pub the night he died—'

'The night we think he died,' Macy put in.

'Yes. The woman he was with that night was an actor, according to Connor, and her name was Rosie. She got to the pub before him and left before him and then he got a call. The next thing we know is a woman's car broke down in that lay-by and his body is found nearby.' She flicked on her indicator to overtake a lorry. 'Well, I've been trying to trace her. There's a Rosie who works at Greenaways but I didn't get a chance to meet her. Anyway, the woman in the pub said she was an actor—'

'And you forgot Stratford, which is probably the only theatre for miles that is still running the same play now as on the eighteenth of June.'

Sometimes Macy surprised her, Jo had to admit. Mind you, it was easy for him to be clever once she had done the hard work.

'I take back what I said about this car only doing seventy,' Macy murmured as Jo sped along in the fast lane of the A46.

Jo waved her hand. 'I like going fast. Don't worry, you're quite safe.' In Stratford high street she had to honk her horn at an ill-behaved coach and neatly cut up a taxi in order to park near the river.

'What do you make of the brother? Connor?' Macy asked.

They walked past the church gates, where the shade was deep enough to make Jo shiver. 'You don't like him, do you?' she said.

'Can you think of anyone I do like?' Macy demanded. 'Liking has nothing to do with it. I don't *believe* him.'

They reached the riverbank and watched the packed pleasure boats narrowly missing the rowers. Macy took the aged sandwich out of its plastic bag and began to break it up for the ducks, who crowded round, greedy and grateful. 'Another thing that doesn't fit your picture of Sean is his financial difficulties,' he added. 'If he was a diligent bank clerk like you make out, why was he so badly in debt?'

'He was a bit more senior than a clerk,' Jo had to point out. 'Anyway I only know he owed Connor money. I must owe my sister money. It's not the same as being in debt.'

'Well, he was,' Macy said. 'Don't forget debt is part of our business too. I've run some checks on Sean Fitzpatrick.

He was known to local debt collectors. Sorry, that's all there is,' he said to the ducks. He turned to stroll beside the river and Jo walked behind him, having to strain to hear what he said as his soft voice did not carry very well. 'Connor also told me after he saw the body. He said he didn't know how bad Sean's debts were but it is in the thousands.'

'He probably gambled it away,' Jo suggested. 'After all, a middle manager's salary from the bank wouldn't go far if you spent most of your nights at casinos. Did you find out anything from those clubs?'

'I made a start. I swallowed my pride and went to see my ex-father-in-law. He runs Diamonds.'

Jo had once spent a boring evening at Diamonds, one of Coventry's few casinos. She filed away for future reference the fact that Macy must have married the daughter of its owner.

'George knew Sean,' Macy said. 'He wasn't exactly a regular but he'd been in now and then. Spent a lot and lost a lot. I'll try the London ones next week. Knowing George is like a letter of introduction.'

They threaded between the clumps of tourists, who seemed to have agreed on a uniform of pale T shirts, bright shorts and selfie sticks. It was more congested as they came closer to the town centre and the brick-built Swan Theatre jutting out across the river. Jo pulled Macy across the grass towards it.

'There's another thing.' Macy, with his hands in his jacket pockets, was obviously more concerned with the disorder in his head than around him. 'Don't you think that Connor is more than a bit edgy?'

'Edgy? Yes, I noticed he seemed nervous when I went to his house.' Jo walked up the theatre steps. 'Come on, I want to go in here.'

They walked into an old-fashioned theatre lobby. The tourists had not neglected the Swan. They were crowded into the shop, which Jo ignored. With Macy following, she went up to a counter. A girl in a baggy jumper smiled at them pleasantly. Jo asked if she had a cast list for the musical that was currently playing.

'Yes, hang on. I do have some.' She ducked down behind the counter for a moment and reappeared with a flyer.

Jo scanned it. 'I'm looking for a friend called Rosie. She said she worked here. Do you know her?'

The girl pulled at the sleeve of her jumper. 'I don't think I do,' she said. 'Sorry. Have you tried the main house? They'll give you cast lists for their productions.'

Jo and Macy retreated into the sunshine. A crowd of Japanese girls swarming around the steps pounced on Macy and asked if he would take a picture of them. Jo watched amused as he tried to get them to stand still while her mind went over what she knew about Rosie. She was not getting anywhere at present. Perhaps that was understandable. If the woman was Sean's murderer, would she really have offered her correct name and occupation to any oik who tried to chat her up?

She sighed. 'One more try.' She led Macy round to the front of the main theatre and through the spacious modern foyer to the box office. Macy looked around furtively as if someone might try to make him sit through three hours of *Henry IV Part Two*.

They waited in the snaking, cordoned queue for a few minutes. Jo repeated her questions at one of the desks in a line of staff, who were more numerous and less patient. She was handed three cast lists wordlessly and the woman called for her next customer. Jo stood to one side, scanning the lists and noticed there was a Rosalind Wynchcombe in *Romeo and Juliet*.

She looked up, but she had already been usurped by the snaking queue of customers. She went up to a young woman who was tidying a stack of books in the shop. She had one of those faces that show a lot of skin, a broad face with hair scraped back from the forehead and wide, flat cheeks. Attractive but not conventionally pretty. Before Jo could form her complicated question about the cast list, her eyes moved back to the badge on the girl's sweatshirt. *RSC Stratford*, it said. *Rosie Martell.*

'Are you Rosie?' Jo asked. Was this the woman who had walked past her in Greenaways yesterday? She wasn't sure.

'Yes,' the girl answered, her expression puzzled but not put out by the question.

'I've been looking for you. Is there any way we can have a word?'

'Looking for me? What do you mean by that?' A wary look crossed Rosie's open face and she brought a hand to her lips for comfort.

'Don't worry. Could I just ask you a few questions? I'll buy us a coffee. I'm a private investigator.' Jo explained.

Rosie stared at her, then turned away to speak to a woman behind the line of desks. 'Do you mind if I go on my break now? I've got to see someone.' The other woman agreed with a brief nod and Rosie turned back to Jo. 'All right, I'll see you in the café in a couple of minutes.'

CHAPTER ELEVEN

'Found someone!' Jo announced triumphantly to Macy when she rejoined him on a bench outside. 'There's a Rosie who works in the shop — or maybe the box office.'

'I thought you were looking for an actor. Or a dancer.'

Jo shrugged. 'Maybe she likes to glamorise her job a bit. Come on, I'm meeting her for coffee in a second.'

Macy and Jo found a table in the narrow café, which looked out over the river. They could have sat on the veranda in the sun but Jo wanted to make sure that Rosie saw them, so they sat with a good view of the doorway, where it was warm, crowded and noisy. Jo bought three coffees with biscuits and they sat in silence, Jo giving every woman who came in a second look. Rosie eventually arrived, wearing a vest and jeans and, looking self-conscious, she weaved between the tables towards them.

'What's all this about?' she asked. 'And who's he?'

Jo waved a hand towards the empty seat. 'Come on, I only want to ask you a couple of things. This is David Macy. He's my boss.'

'Just ignore me. I thought I was off duty today.' Macy gave Rosie a quick smile and she sat down.

'What, are you really private investigators?' Rosie looked from Jo to Macy. 'You must be following some poor woman's husband, are you? Well my conscience is clear on that score.' She gave a grin. 'Why do you want to see me? Is it someone I know?'

Macy interrupted Jo's intended explanation. 'Well, it's not that sort of thing but it is a bit confidential. Have you worked here long?'

'Three months. It's just one of my part-time summer jobs,' Rosie said.

'What do you do the rest of the time?' Macy asked, giving her all his attention. Jo was irritated and amused by his obvious flirting. She would have gone about the interview in a more straightforward way but, observing the success Macy was having, she stayed quiet.

'You'll never guess.' Rosie took a preliminary sip at the froth on her coffee. 'Go on.'

'A librarian,' Macy suggested.

Rosie looked at Jo. 'Is he joking or what?'

'Just ignore him,' Jo advised.

'Actually I'm a dancer,' Rosie announced. 'A professional. But I have to do another job to maintain my standard of living. You know how it is.' She sipped more coffee and smiled at Macy. 'So what do you want, then? Who's this naughty husband you're following? Go on, you can tell me.'

'Sean Fitzpatrick,' Jo answered.

Rosie's mascara-covered lashes flickered over her coffee cup. She replaced the cup on its saucer and turned her face to Jo. 'Who?' she said. 'I've never heard of him.'

Jo had never been more convinced someone was lying. 'You see, we are being paid to find out why he died,' she said matter-of-factly.

'Oh, really.' Rosie's eyes wandered around the café and she looked noticeably less assured. She brought her gaze back to Macy. 'Funny job you do.'

'Pays the bills.' Macy shrugged. 'You didn't know this Sean, then?'

'No. Should I? I meet lots of people. Have you got a picture?'

Jo produced her phone with the familiar photograph. Rosie studied it and shook her head. 'So he's dead, is he? How did he die?'

'He was hit over the head and left in a wood near Draycote Water. Near the Castaway,' Jo explained, and then took a new tack. 'It's a pub — not far away — between Leamington and Coventry. Do you know it?'

'Vaguely. I might have been there once or twice. I think they have barbecues sometimes.'

'Do you remember going last month? About two weeks ago?' Jo asked.

Rosie laughed, a peal of real amusement that made people look round. 'My God,' she said. 'I have trouble remembering the pub I went to last night, let alone two weeks ago.'

'Someone saw you there with this man on the eighteenth of June,' Jo said. 'It was a Friday.'

Rosie looked concerned. 'Did they? This is a bit serious, isn't it? If they go around telling the police that, I'll be at the bloody police station answering questions before you know it. Who's making these things up?'

'I can't say,' Jo answered. 'We haven't told the police anything. We're only interested because we're trying to find out what happened to Sean that night. Were you there?'

Rosie shook her head. 'No. I know where I was on the eighteenth because Fridays are my dance practice nights. You can ask my partner Dean Hampton if you like. He's been my partner for the last three years and we practise twice a week at the moment for the Midlands Championships—'

'Oh, that sort of dancing,' Macy interrupted again. 'Ballroom dancing, isn't it? You must be quite good to get into the Midlands Cup.' Rosie looked at him in surprise, which Jo felt probably mirrored her own expression.

'We've been finalists the last two years but never won. Anyway—' she tossed her ponytail over her shoulder and stood up — 'I'll have to go back now. It's the end of my break. Thanks for the coffee and the warning. I'll try not to bump into any policemen for a while. It looks like someone's got me mixed up with someone else.'

Macy got up to walk back with her. 'By the way — do you ever say you're an actor?'

'Actually I do act a bit.' Rosie nodded. 'Mainly I'm a dancer, though.'

'Do you work at Greenaways as well? The sports club in Leamington?' Jo butted in, determined not to let Macy take over completely.

'No. Look, I've got to get back now—'

'Just tell us your number so we can get in touch. Please?' Jo added.

Rosie rattled off a telephone number, which had Jo scrabbling in her bag for a pen and paper.

She wrote quickly. The meeting had felt like a bit of a disappointment after all that searching for her. This might be her last chance to ask Rosie anything. 'Hold on a minute.'

The girl paused outside the box office.

'Just one more thing. What car do you drive?'

She shook her head and said she couldn't afford a car. 'Ask Dean if you don't believe me. He works at Cassidy's, the bar in Coventry,' she said over her shoulder. She seemed unconcerned. 'He'll be able to tell you where I was that night.'

Jo and Macy left the theatre and walked back to the car.

'That flirting was so blatant, you know,' Jo complained.

'I thought she was rather blatant with me actually,' he said. 'Anyway it worked, didn't it? What would you have done?'

'I would have tried to get her on my side. As it is, we didn't get much out of her. I'm sure she knew who Sean was. And she could have been the girl I saw in Greenaways but I'm not sure. But then why would she say she didn't work there? That seems a pointless sort of lie. It's so easy for us to check.'

Macy had to agree with her about that. They were passing a pub and he suggested a drink.

Jo smiled as another idea occurred to her. 'I wouldn't mind,' she said, 'but that place is full of tourists. What about trying Cassidy's?'

Macy pointed out that if Rosie was at all concerned about her alibi she would have rung her friend Dean to warn him to back her up but by then Jo was already driving them in the direction of Coventry.

The bar was in a converted bank — one of those banks that was built in the days when they tried to look safe and impressive instead of fashionable and friendly. It was vast inside and the few people sitting around over their phones or idly chatting were dwarfed by the great pillars and sweeping central staircase. Jo and Macy sat down roughly where she used to queue to pay off her credit card debts. *That was when I could afford debts*, Jo thought ruefully.

Macy mused aloud, gazing at the fancy plaster ceiling. 'You know, on reflection, I might disagree with you about our interview with Rosie. I think that, in trying to tell us nothing, she actually revealed quite a bit about herself.'

Jo quelled the urge to take issue with this and contented herself with saying, 'Well, I suppose at least we both agree she was not being straight with us.'

A waiter approached and they both had to concentrate on the menu. Although the place was not crowded, he strode up, whipped a cloth over the table and stood over them with tablet poised. He treated any signs of dithering with such silent contempt that Jo ended up ordering the deep-fried calamari rings against her better judgement.

'Is Dean here?' Jo asked before the stocky man could rush off. She was fairly confident he was not a dancer. He moved more like a rugby centre-forward.

'I'll get him.' The waiter headed back to the bar.

'Certainly can't complain about the slow service,' Macy remarked.

A tall, slight boy brought Macy's beer and Jo's cappuccino. He looked younger than Rosie, maybe just twenty, Jo thought. He placed the glasses down with a till receipt and regarded them through curtains of blonde hair, which fell from a central parting. He obviously knew they had asked for him and was waiting to find out why.

'Are you Rosie Martell's dance partner?' Jo asked.

'Yes,' Dean answered. He was cautious but not startled by the question. Perhaps Rosie had called him to warn him as Macy had suggested.

'Ballroom dancing, isn't it?' Macy said. 'What type do you do? You know, Latin American or what?'

'Mainly modern in competitions.' Dean looked at Macy through narrowed eyes. 'Why? Have you seen us dance?'

'No, we've just been speaking to Rosie,' Jo explained. She felt a bit sorry for Dean. And she didn't want Macy to hijack another interview. 'We wanted to know where she was on the eighteenth of June.'

Dean ran a cloth along some spilt beer on the table and spoke without looking at Jo. 'If it was a Friday or a Tuesday in the last six weeks, she was with me. Why do you want to know that?'

'Someone said they saw her in the Castaway. Do you know it?' Dean shook his head. 'It's a pub near Leamington. The same night a man was killed near there. His name was Sean Fitzpatrick. Have you ever heard of him? Or has Rosie ever mentioned him?'

'Don't think so.' Dean moved away from the table as if trying to literally keep them at arm's length. But he didn't walk away altogether. 'You're not the police though, are you? So why do you want to know?' He tapped the empty tray against his leg in a repetitive movement.

'We were asked to find Sean. His brother was concerned about him. Now it turns out he's dead, his brother's even more concerned,' Jo explained.

Dean shook his head again. 'It's nothing to do with me and Rosie. We see a lot of each other at the moment because we're practising really hard for the championships. It's very important. I'm sure Rosie wouldn't get involved with anything that might get in the way.' He stopped as if anxious he might have said too much.

Jo felt even sorrier for him but what he said had been useful. What if these championships did mean a lot to Rosie and Sean had somehow got in the way? Was that ridiculously far-fetched? 'How long do you practise?' she asked.

'Three hours. Seven till ten. At least,' he added. He glanced around, shaking back his blonde curtains. 'I've got to go now.'

'Where could we see you dance?' Macy asked. 'I'm very interested in ballroom dancing.'

The boy hesitated. 'Really?' he said with a forced smile. 'In a month's time our club is doing an exhibition at the Leofric Hotel. You won't need tickets, just turn up. Formal dress, though, I'm afraid.' He threw a little departing glance at Macy's clothes and walked away with more confidence than when he had arrived.

'I don't believe either of them,' Jo remarked to Macy over her coffee. For some reason both Rosie and Dean made her feel uneasy.

Macy's look was quizzical. 'What can we do about it?'

Jo did not have an answer to this at present, so she turned to another subject that was bothering her. 'Have you ever heard of Kelly Greenaway? She's the woman who owns that club I went to last night.'

Macy frowned. 'There's something familiar about the name — I'll look it up when I get back to the office. Of course, I could have done that before you went if you'd kept me informed. I'm always the last person to know anything that happens—'

Jo wasn't listening. She was admiring the fancy gold plasterwork on the ceiling and wondering if Dean and Rosie were covering for each other.

CHAPTER TWELVE

Jo told herself it was ridiculous to be nervous about an interview for a job she didn't even want, but waiting to be called into the second interview at the bank brought back those months of desperate job-hunting, when she had been trying to convince potential employers that her experience of travelling halfway round the world made her an asset to them. It didn't help either that her face was still showing the results of Saturday night's scrap with Rupert the Dobermann.

She was sipping the obligatory lukewarm coffee when Vaz came over to her. 'Nick is ready to see you now.'

His manner is cool today, Jo thought, as she was led past Sean Fitzpatrick's office. It still had his name on the door and she couldn't resist staring in. *What would I find in there?* she wondered. *Would an inspection of his office reveal more about the elusive Sean?* She saw Vaz frowning at her and smiled back at him blandly.

Nick Walmsley had wonderful eyelashes. It was not the first thing Jo noticed but it was the most memorable. He was short and slight and seemed at home in his sizeable office. His handshake and his welcome were warm and definite. 'Jo.' He smiled as if he had known her all his life. 'How are you?'

Jo sat down and fielded the usual questions intended to put her at her ease. She concentrated not so much on her answers as on Nick himself, whom she found interesting. His suit and tie were sober and his light brown hair was neat. His hands remained clasped loosely in front of him but she sensed a suppressed energy about him. He conducted the interview in an affable, informal style.

Jo went through her prepared answers and it was difficult to know whether Nick Walmsley was impressed or not. He remained friendly throughout. His pleasant, deep-set eyes were difficult to read. At the end he asked if she had any questions and Jo took the chance to find out more about Sean Fitzpatrick.

'If I got the job, would I be working for Mr Fitzpatrick?' she asked.

Nick's smile did not alter but he shook his head. 'Afraid not. He's not with the bank anymore. Do you know him well?' There was a fraction of a hesitation over the question. Nick must be guessing she didn't know about Sean's death and deciding it wasn't worth explaining.

'No, but he recommended the job to me,' Jo said. 'I believe he liked working here and thought it would suit me too.'

Nick gave a short laugh, which Jo wished she understood. 'Did he say that? Well, feedback is a gift, isn't it?' He did not elaborate but glanced at his watch, shuffled his papers and politely brought the interview to a close. Jo noted the obligatory framed photograph of his wife and kids on the side of his desk, though he wore no rings. Here was Mr National Commercial Bank of the year, surely, she thought. And yet there was something about him which did not quite fit the image.

He led her out of the office. 'One thing's for sure. If you do start work for the bank, there's no shortage of work for you.' His PA was stationed at her desk nearby. 'This is Carol, she'll show you out. With two members of staff absent, work is building up all the time, isn't it, Carol?'

'Certainly is,' Carol agreed. 'It's been chaos here the last few weeks, what with the auditors coming and going. Thank goodness that's over, but I don't know how we're going to do without Sean and Cass. They had Securities taped between them. And your inbox is going bonkers, Nick. I don't know when I'm going to get round to sorting the emails.'

'Don't worry,' Nick placated her. 'You know what I always say: it's all under control.' He flashed a grin at Jo. 'Sometimes people are silly enough to believe it. Thanks for coming in.' He shook hands again and went back into his office.

'You can't fool me, I've known you too long,' Carol called after him. 'He fools everybody else though,' she confided to Jo. 'Nick is the exec's darling. Can't do a thing wrong. My only hope is they keep promoting me alongside him so I get to be an EA before I'm 30 — that's the goal and it's worked so far.' Jo wasn't entirely sure what an EA was but muttered something supportive about it being good to have a target.

Carol led Jo back through the office, walking briskly ahead in her sensible loafers. She was well-dressed but Jo considered her clothes too middle-aged, guessing that the woman was only about her own age. She thought she may as well get as much out of the talkative Carol as possible. 'I expect you've heard the news about Sean Fitzpatrick?'

'Oh yes, isn't it terrible? Did you know him? I know it's an awful thing to say but, in a way, I wasn't surprised. Shocked, yes, but not really *surprised*. Do you know what I mean?' Carol pressed the lift button. 'I'll need to take your day pass off you.'

'I think so. Of course, I only knew him slightly.' Jo took the coloured lanyard over her head and handed it back to Carol.

'I've had to see the police about him, actually. They've taken over an interview room on the seventh floor and they want to see everyone who had anything to do with Sean.'

'Really? What did they want to know?' Jo tried to sound like she was asking out of idle curiosity.

'Oh, endless things.' Carol folded her arms over her floral print dress. 'How long have I known him, was he any good at this job and suchlike. I tried to be diplomatic.' She paused to chew her lipstick. 'But you never know what conclusions they're drawing. Do you know what I mean?'

They stepped into the lift. 'I can imagine,' Jo sympathised. 'It sounds a bit harrowing. They wanted to know everything about Sean, then?'

'Yes. They asked if I'd had any leave in the last couple of weeks — which I haven't because it's been too busy. And what did I do the last two weekends? I said not much, I was too knackered after working at this place all week. It's been dire lately, it really has. They said he'd last been seen alive on a Friday two weeks ago. Creepy, isn't it?' The enclosed lift space seemed to make Carol even more inclined to chat.

'How could anyone remember what they were doing on any one day like that?' Jo put in. 'I'm sure I couldn't.'

'Ah, well, Fridays are easy, you see. Friday nights Nick and I always work late because we're doing the reports for Monday prayers. That's a stupid name for it—' she grinned at Jo — 'but if you work here you'll get used to that. Hundreds of acronyms and stupid names. Prayers is what they call the first meeting of the week. It's a three-line whip — that means everybody must attend. All the senior leaders, anyway, which means that it's quite normal for us both to be here until seven or eight o'clock on Fridays.'

'You too? That's devotion to duty.'

'Tell me about it. People think being a PA is just emails but really my role is more of a business manager. I'm lucky with Nick as I have a boss that gives me those opportunities, of course.' Carol glanced across at her as the lift came to rest on the ground floor. 'Half the time, I'm doing Nick's work.'

Jo was reluctant to step out of the lift. Carol was a mine of information. 'You must know Nick very well.'

'I've been working for him for five years. He has his quirks — they all do. But he's good for my career and I can't argue with that.'

'What about Sean? He doesn't seem to have been as popular?' Jo followed Carol across the atrium towards the security desk, where she handed Jo's pass over and signed her out. Being observed by the uniformed woman behind the desk didn't deter the PA from giving her opinion.

'To me, Sean never was right for the bank at all. He used to like a few too many cocktails and bets on the gee-gees — and he always seemed to me to be just on the brink of trouble. I sound heartless, don't I? Still, it comes to us all in the end. Only not so unpleasantly, I hope.' She chuckled and added with a knowing look, 'You never know, we may see each other again soon.'

Jo was sorry to wave goodbye to Carol as she walked back to the lift. She had found out more from her in five minutes than a whole week of work on the investigation. However she didn't have much choice but to head across the wide atrium for the exit and then the train. But while she was walking slowly away from the front desk, she began to wonder. Would anyone notice if she went back to have a look in Sean's office?

The only people likely to recognise her were Carol, Nick and Vaz. Nick would be interviewing the next candidate, she assumed. She would have to hope Carol stayed near Nick's office, which she wouldn't have to pass. Vaz had been working so diligently, with his head down over his desk, that she would be unlucky if he happened to glance up and see her.

In full view of the uniformed reception staff, Jo started to empty her bag and check her pockets. After a minute or two of this performance, she returned to the desk and announced that she had left her phone upstairs. 'I've left it in the ladies,' she said. She pointed to her visitor's badge, which was still lying in the tray. 'I was being interviewed and was on the point of leaving when I realised. Do you mind if I go and fetch it?'

The request produced a short, quiet confab between the man and woman who shared the desk. She realised they might call Carol, who would offer to go and look for the phone, which of course she wouldn't find. *Could be awkward,* Jo thought and was already contemplating suddenly rediscovering her phone when a small group of people entered the building and demanded attention.

The woman handed her pass back to her before she attended to the group. 'Be quick. Ten minutes max.'

As soon as she was in the lift, Jo took off her lanyard and dropped it into her pocket. She decided it made her look more conspicuous, and the only way to get away with this plan was brazenly.

She strolled out of the lift holding her head high and pushed through the swing doors. She walked past one of the other interviewees, who was sitting on the edge of the easy chair. Seeing an apparently neglected blue file on a nearby desk, Jo picked it up and stuck it prominently under her arm. Sean's door still stood ajar. The office was nearer Vaz's desk than she had remembered but his chair was empty. She looked round and couldn't see him so she took her chance, walked swiftly across to Sean's door and slipped in.

She closed the door behind her and made for the desk. It was clear apart from some abandoned cables and a calendar. She tried the left drawer. Locked. The right drawer. Also locked.

She turned to the cabinet behind the desk. It opened but it only seemed to contain some stationery and files that didn't mean anything to her. This was getting her nowhere. She sighed and wondered why she had ever thought this was a good idea. Any useful information would be digital and if she couldn't get on to a system, she wouldn't find anything. She glanced at the computer, and knew it was not even worth switching it on.

She looked around the room for inspiration. There were no family pictures in this office. Either Sean had possessed austere tastes or the police had removed anything personal. Probably the latter, Jo guessed. In another cupboard she found a half-empty bottle of Scotch and a glass, a single coffee mug and an opened bag of sugar. Sean was clearly not one for office hospitality.

Her phone, now clutched in her slightly sweaty hand, told her she had only been in Sean's room three minutes. She was reluctant to give up but she couldn't see anywhere else to search in the bare room. Then she lifted her head slightly and noticed a cardboard box on top of the cupboard behind the desk. It was pushed to the back so it was not clearly visible. She stood on a swivel chair and reached on top of the cupboard.

'My God! What are you *doing*?'

Jo swung round and the chair beneath her nearly did an extra revolution. She clung to the top of the cupboard for safety. It shuddered. For a horrible moment she thought the whole lot was going to come down on top of her. She steadied herself, trying to maintain some panache. 'I'm trying to get this box down,' she said, for once deciding that honesty was the best policy.

Vaz looked outraged and anxious. 'I thought you'd left,' he said. But at least he was still keeping his voice down. Jo thought such presence of mind was promising. With some difficulty, she got one arm around the cardboard box and began a tricky descent.

Vaz did not come to help her out. 'Did you know Sean Fitzpatrick is dead? You can't go messing about with his private things. You know the police are here, don't you?' He watched as Jo put the box on the desk and started to rummage around in it. 'Security will have you out of here in thirty seconds,' he said, but she sensed he was more puzzled than angry now.

'I'm a private investigator,' she explained, somewhat breathlessly. 'I'm not here for the job, I'm looking into Sean's death. You do know he was murdered?' She pulled out some old copies of the *Financial Times* and peered at the dates: 16, 17 and 18 June. They were folded open on the markets page and some share prices were circled in blue pen.

'I heard rumours,' Vaz said. 'I didn't know for sure. Look, you can't stay in here—'

Jo sighed over the papers. 'I suppose everyone who works in a bank has got shares in something or other. It doesn't mean much that Sean has circled these companies, does it?'

'What companies are they?' Vaz came over to the desk and looked at the paper. Jo had to hide a smile. Somehow she had always felt he would be on her side. 'Cereals, oil, retailing,' he muttered. 'No significance that I can see. Investing on the stock market was a bit of a hobby with Sean, I think. He probably moved his shares about most days.'

Jo reached further into the box. She had found two bottles of pills. She scribbled down the names so she could find out later why Sean was taking medication. There was also a squash racket and some smelly old trainers. 'What is all this stuff?' she said, mainly to herself.

'I told you. They're his personal things. The ones the police didn't take. I put them in a box. I'm going to offer them to his next of kin when I get round to it. I believe he has a brother.'

'Yes, that's who I'm working for. I can take this box to him if you like,' Jo said.

Vaz was not having this. 'No. I'm keeping it here for the time being. The police may come back for it. Look, you'll have to go,' he said. He glanced around desperately and then turned his worried face to Jo. 'I've got something for you that might help. But you must promise to leave if I give it to you.' Jo agreed. 'Wait a minute and stay out of sight.'

Jo did as she was told and hid behind the door.

'It's quiet out there now,' he said when he came back in. 'Most people are at lunch. It's a good time to get you out.' He handed her a piece of paper with a name, address and telephone number on it. 'Get in touch with Cass. She might be able to help you. And for heaven's sake, put your pass on.'

'Why? Who is she?' Jo pulled her pass over her head and allowed Vaz to lead her out. Trying to look as business-like as possible, they walked side by side towards the lifts.

'She's the girl whose job you've just been interviewed for,' Vaz answered while they waited for the lift to arrive. 'Don't ask me too many questions. I want to stay out of it. Just go and see her.'

Unfortunately for Jo, there was someone else in the lift, so she couldn't question him further until they reached the ground floor. Vaz, apparently determined to see her safely off the premises, accompanied her back to the desk, where she meekly thanked the receptionist and left her pass. She could almost feel the intensity of Vaz's relief as she walked away.

CHAPTER THIRTEEN

Jo tried Cass's number at the first coffee shop she came to. People hurrying past clutching cardboard cups and paper bags of food had made her realise she was hungry and she had tagged on to the end of a queue. She studied the blackboard above the counter, while listening to Cass's number ring out. *Not very promising*, she thought. Could Vaz have been just fobbing her off? She had no idea why he should choose to help her but decided it was still worth putting some effort into finding the woman.

The sandwich shop was another of those places where she felt under pressure to choose and if she wasn't careful she would end up with either something hideous like a crabmeat and beetroot sandwich or something boring like cheese and pickle. She had only read about a quarter of the blackboard by the time the woman behind the counter looked in her direction. Staying cool under pressure from the restive queue behind her, Jo chose a baguette filled with Brie and grapes and an Americano.

She ate it standing up, leaning against a minuscule table in an ambience about as relaxed as a station waiting room where everyone was expecting their train to be announced. She tried Cass's number again with no luck and studied the maps on her phone to see how long it would take to get to her address. By the time she was halfway through her baguette, she had decided she needed to take the overground train to Stonebridge, which was somewhere near Wembley.

After the short journey, she had to consult her phone again and, when she was sure where she was going, she set off down a road that seemed to be a row of small shops punctuated by high-rise blocks of flats. She turned into a narrower road where every other shop seemed to be a betting shop. One unfamiliar supermarket had windows covered with wire mesh and groups of people standing around outside who avoided eye contact. Jo walked past a pub with a very loud television shouting from the dark bar. A group of men standing outside with glasses in their hands made the most of Jo's passing to alleviate their boredom.

When she turned left again, she stopped in the next shop doorway for a quick glance at the phone screen. This was the kind of area where she wanted to look like she knew where she was going so she memorised the next few directions and zipped the phone into her bag. With only one wrong turning, she ended up in the right street and walked past another bookies, a newsagents and an off-licence, looking for Cass's house. Virtually everyone who passed her stared at her, which did not make her feel any more comfortable.

She soon found it — a tall town house with walls that had once been painted white, and steps up to a porch tiled with marked and cracked quarry tiles. Beside the large, peeling front door was a cluster of doorbells, some with names stuck on with yellowing tape beside them. Jo scanned them for a 'C Baxter', but Cass's name wasn't there. Eventually she rang one of the unnamed bells and waited. After trying three more bells, she finally heard promising shuffling noises from inside.

A woman about a foot shorter than Jo opened the door. She was elderly and faded. It took Jo a little while to establish that a girl who could be Cass had just moved into the top flat.

'Been chucked out by some man, I expect,' the older woman remarked, opening the door wider so Jo could step into the damp-smelling hall. Jo looked around at the aged mustard carpet and the inevitable mound of mail and flyers on a flimsy table. She was just about to start up the stairs when the woman leaned towards her. 'What do you want her for?'

'I've just come on behalf of a colleague to see how she's getting on,' Jo said.

'This girl doesn't work. I've never seen her leave this house yet except to get cigarettes and food.'

And I bet she wouldn't get by without you noticing, Jo thought. The woman watched her start to climb the stairs and shuffled off to her ground-floor flat. Jo heard a blast from the radio as she opened the door. It was an old house, though, and the sound did not travel once the door was closed. Jo carried on up the steep stairs. At each landing was a bathroom and toilet. She happened to glance in the open door of one and wished she hadn't.

The flat at the top was number eight. There was no mention of a number on the piece of paper Vaz had given her and Jo was doubtful that she had found the right place. She tapped tentatively at the door. There was no answer.

She knocked harder. Still no answer. But it didn't feel like an empty silence. She waited and knocked again. She was sure she heard some movement but still no reply.

'Is Cass Baxter there?' Jo called. Her voice sounded hollow on the empty landing. She waited and listened to nothing at all. 'Vaz gave me your address. He said you might be able to help me.' She paused again. There was no response. 'I'm trying to find out what happened to Sean Fitzpatrick. You knew him, didn't you?' Jo left a long gap before going on. 'In fact, I was interviewed for your job this morning—'

'You can stick the job up your arse,' came a belligerent voice from surprisingly close to the door.

'I don't want the job,' Jo retorted. 'I only went there in the first place to find out about Sean. Open the door, I want to ask a couple of questions about him.'

'Why do you want to know?' came the same aggressive voice.

'I'll tell you when you open the door,' she answered.

'Piss off.'

She was almost inclined to take this advice. Her first impression of Cass Baxter didn't encourage her to get better acquainted. She moved away from the door and thought about one more question. 'Why did you leave the bank?'

'Why do you want to know?' the truculent voice demanded.

'I'm not explaining it through a bloody door,' Jo called back. 'If you want to know why I'm here, open up.'

'You're not the police, are you?'

'No. I don't think they would hang around while you decided whether or not you were going to let them in.'

Whether this logic or persistence won, Jo never bothered to wonder, but Cass did finally open the door a grudging six inches. Jo could barely make out a slim figure with long hair and long clothes.

'Can I come in?' Jo asked more patiently, wondering if she had to put on a repeat performance before progressing any further. But Cass only hesitated half a minute.

'All right. If you must.' She held the door wider. 'Only it's not exactly the *Ideal Home* exhibition in here and I've got no tea.'

'It's all right, I don't like tea.'

Jo walked past Cass into the flat. It was a studio, in fact, and amounted to one small room with no division marking off the cooking area from the sleeping area. It had a single long, narrow sash window and was untidy and not very clean. There were two cardboard boxes and a suitcase on the floor. Another lay open on the single bed with clothes tumbling out of it.

'Only just moved in?' Jo asked. She looked up at Cass, who was still standing by the door. She was thin and scruffy, with unbrushed fair hair hanging either side of her face. It had been highlighted with cheap reddish dye, which made her face look pale. Her dress was long and floral, the kind of thing she could possibly have worn at the bank but not with the ancient woolly cardigan hanging down to her knees and the men's grey socks she had on.

'A week ago. Dump, isn't it?' Cass said. She reached for her cigarette, which was lying on a saucer. She inhaled while taking a sidelong look at Jo through the long fringe.

'I've come to ask you some questions about Sean,' Jo said, 'but I know so little about him I don't really know where to start.' She looked out of the window to avoid staring either at Cass or the place. The view of waste ground being used as a car park was dispiriting.

Cass said nothing.

Jo sighed. 'All I know is, he worked for a bank, his brother's called Connor, who is a charmer I can't fathom out. I didn't like his mother—'

'Me neither,' Cass put in unexpectedly. 'Stuck up cow, talking down her nose and looking like she'd just stepped out of *Woman and Home*.'

Jo laughed. 'More like *Country Living*, if you ask me. Anyway, I just need to know anything you can tell me about Sean.'

Cass hadn't moved except to put her cigarette to her lips but she lifted her head to regard Jo more openly. Her face was white, undernourished and unhealthy-looking, but she had attractive blue eyes and delicate features.

'I'm with you now.' Cass regarded Jo with some sympathy. 'You're another of his cast-offs, aren't you?' She leaned down to stub her cigarette out on the saucer.

Jo didn't answer. An uncomfortable suspicion had drifted into her mind.

Cass went on bitterly, 'He knows how to hump 'em and dump 'em, does Sean. I knew that before I got involved. Stupid cow that I am. He always was a bastard and he'll never change, I'll tell you that much.'

Now Jo was sure. Cass didn't know he was dead. Jo didn't relish telling her but it had to be done. 'Actually,' Jo began, 'I'm not here because I was involved with him—'

'Well don't. That's my advice. Sean absolutely loves himself and no one else gets a look-in. Thinks he is the smartest, brightest bastard that ever lived. You know how he's always impressing you with how he got one over on somebody—' Cass came to a halt. 'Hang on. Have I got it all wrong as usual?'

'Well . . . I don't know how to tell you this. For some reason I thought you already knew. You see, Sean's dead.'

Cass brought clenched hands to her face. Her eyes seemed to grow even larger.

'And what makes it worse,' Jo went on, 'he was murdered.'

'How? When?' Cass moved her hands to her mouth.

'He was hit over the head and buried in a shallow grave. The police haven't found the weapon as far as I know. It was in the middle of June.'

Cass swore. She stumbled towards the bed and sat on a pile of underwear. 'I suppose I ought to be pleased,' she muttered. 'I've wished him dead often enough. Christ only knows he deserves to be dead.'

'I'll get you something to drink.' Jo made her way over to the kitchen area.

'I've told you, I've got no tea,' Cass said, her voice rising hysterically.

'There must be something else.' Jo opened empty dirty cupboards and an entirely bare fridge. There didn't seem to be any food at all.

'For Christ's sake, come and sit down!' Cass yelled. 'I told you there was nothing to drink.' She began to cry, still trying to take drags on her cigarette in between sobs and talking incoherently about Sean. Jo went over to try to comfort her and in the process managed to knock over a half-empty bottle of beer beside the bed. By the time she had found a cloth to mop it up, Cass had recovered a bit.

'It's all right. You wouldn't notice against this carpet anyway,' Cass said. It did seem that the beer had sunk in without trace on the lurid patterned carpet. Jo abandoned the job.

'I had a nice place, you know.' Cass wiped her face on a towel from the suitcase. 'A flat in Notting Hill. I just couldn't afford the mortgage once I'd left the bank. I finally dropped the keys in the door of the building society the other night.'

'Why did you leave the bank? Because of Sean?' Jo asked.

'Vaz didn't tell you that, then?' Cass looked up. Her face was blotched but her eyes were dry now. 'I gave him this address because he insisted I keep in touch. He's a nice bloke. He was the only one who really seemed to care when Sean got me the sack.'

'Sean got you sacked from the bank? What do you mean?' Jo asked. Then, seeing Cass's streaky, grimy face, she added, 'Look, tell me about you and Sean and why you left the bank over a cup of tea. Is there somewhere we can go?'

'There's a café not too far away that does good buttered toast.' Cass blew her nose on the towel. 'I suppose we could go there. It would get us out of this hole for a bit.'

Jo was equally keen to leave the depressing room. She waited while Cass washed her face and found some shoes. They went downstairs and left the house, watched, no doubt, by the woman who had let Jo in. Still smoking, Cass seemed more prepared to talk now but she wanted to know why Jo was interested in Sean. The fact that she was a private investigator brought no reaction from Cass, who was still preoccupied with Sean's death.

'It's hard to believe that he is actually not here anymore. Even though I never saw him, at least I knew he was on the same planet . . .' Cass said. 'What's difficult to swallow is that he was daft enough to get himself murdered. Sean always believed he could outsmart anybody, but someone must have borne a grudge, mustn't they?'

The café Cass had chosen was basic but clean. Jo ordered tea and toast for Cass and coffee for herself. 'When did you have to leave the bank?'

Cass took a bite out of the toast. 'Six weeks ago. It makes things worse, being sacked, because without a decent reference I can't get another job.'

'Surely it's pretty difficult for one manager to get someone sacked?'

'He said I'd stolen a hundred and twenty pounds. He said he'd had the cash in his jacket pocket. His jacket was hanging on the back of the chair in his office. I was always in and out of that room so he knew I would be one of the suspects. He reported the money missing to Nick Walmsley.'

'I met Nick this morning. He interviewed me,' Jo put in.

Cass shook her head. 'Thick as thieves, Sean and Nick are. Or were. I wouldn't be surprised if Nick knew that Sean had set me up. He didn't waste any time calling the bank police in.'

'The bank police?'

'I know, it sounds like something out of Ukraine, doesn't it? But the NCB has its own police to investigate crimes among the staff. Banks take money very seriously,' Cass added with a glimmer of humour.

Jo began to like Cass, instead of just feeling sorry for her. Cass poured herself another cup of tea and took a few sips before going on. 'To cut a long story short, the bank police found the cash in my make-up bag. End of one brilliant career.'

'And Sean put it there?' Jo asked, not sure whether to believe this or not. 'Why would he do that?'

'Sean put it in there that morning before we went to work. I was staying over at his place, which I usually did. He probably waited until I went to put my coat on and slipped it into the inside pocket of my make-up bag. It was a risk because I might have seen it if I had touched up my make-up before the police found it there. But Sean liked risks. That would have added to the fun of it for him.'

'And he knew you took your make-up to work and where you kept it?'

'That's right. Maybe he even told the police to have a particularly careful look in my desk because I had money problems.' Cass gave a short laugh. 'That would be a joke, when he was always the one who was thousands in debt.'

'But why would he do it?'

Cass shrugged. 'To get rid of me,' she said simply. 'He was fed up with me. I was past my use-by date. I was getting too involved, wanting to see more of him, asking him where he got to when he wasn't with me. That sort of thing. I could tell he thought I was too clingy, but I just couldn't help myself.' She shook her head and sniffled.

Jo shook her head and stared at Cass. 'I can't believe he would do something so drastic just to finish the relationship. Why not invite you down the pub and tell you he had found someone else or other tried and tested methods?'

'That was part of the problem, you see. My jealousy. I was sure he was seeing someone else and I really gave him a hard time about it. That's why he got fed up with me.' Cass looked at Jo. 'And I was so childish about it. That was what really pissed him off. I used to go through his pockets looking for evidence of the other woman and I even stole his notebook because I was sure I'd find her name and number in there. I should have accepted that was the way he was . . .' Cass's voice tailed off miserably.

'No, you shouldn't,' Jo put in. 'He sounds a—' she paused in the middle of her diatribe as something occurred to her — 'Hold on, did you say you stole his notebook?'

'Yes. I know that was stupid. I don't know what I expected to find. I couldn't tell which of the women in there was the one he was seeing. Or maybe he was screwing all of them. I did think of ringing them all up at one point, that's how bad I got.'

'I don't suppose you've still got the book?' Jo asked. Inwardly, she was sure her sudden instinct was right and willed Cass to say yes.

Cass took a last sip of tea and hunted around in her capacious straw bag. Jo watched, riveted. After a moment Cass pulled out a slim black book with gold-edged pages. 'This is it.'

Jo took it, saying nothing. She was sure that this was the real reason Cass had been sacked before she even looked in it. There was nothing in the names and addresses to confirm her suspicion. It was just a list of people, most of whom lived in London, and whose names she didn't recognise.

'Do you know any of these people?' she asked, continuing to turn the pages. Cass shook her head and Jo sighed. The book wasn't indexed and the addresses were not in any obvious order. It was less than half-full. Jo flicked through empty pages, frowning. Then, near the back, she found a list of numbers. She showed them to Cass. 'What are these?'

Cass stopped rubbing her nose with her palm and looked at the book. 'Account numbers,' she said. 'And sort codes.'

'I thought so. Whose account numbers? They couldn't all have been Sean's, could they?' There were about fifteen numbers in a neat line down the page.

'Doubt it.'

'Wait a minute. You're still on speaking terms with Vaz, aren't you?'

'Yes, I rang him just the other day to give him my new address. Why?'

Jo took out her phone and handed it to Cass. 'Phone Vaz.'

Cass looked bemused. 'Fuck me if I know what his number is, do I?' She pushed Jo's phone away. 'Anyway, I've got my own phone thanks. Things aren't that bad.' She pulled out a mobile from her straw bag, scrolled through her contacts and tapped a number. While it rang, she drank more tea. Whether it was the tea or toast, the colour was coming back into her cheeks a touch.

'Hi, Vaz. It's Cass. I'm with a nutcase who wants to know about Sean. Apparently you sent her.'

Cass listened for a minute or two with the flicker of a smile and then handed the phone to Jo.

'What's going on?' Vaz demanded. 'Is Cass OK? I didn't expect you to go round there—'

'Don't worry, Vaz. She's fine. We've had a cup of tea and I think we might be able to help her at least get a decent reference from the bank. Will you help?' Beside her, Cass twisted her neck to read the list of account numbers in Sean's notebook.

'What are you on about?' Vaz asked, pouring cold water on Jo's excitement. 'I can't write Cass a reference.'

'No. I just want you to check out some account numbers for me. It may prove Cass was right about Sean getting her the sack. Can you do that reasonably easily?'

Vaz hesitated. 'What are these accounts? What do you want to know?'

This temporarily threw Jo as she had not thought it out this far. 'Just who the account belongs to, how much money is in it, that sort of thing,' she said. Eventually, after Cass had added her pleas, Vaz agreed to run a check on the account numbers but said it would have to wait until most people had left the office. Jo said she would ring him back tomorrow morning.

'Of course, nothing may come of it,' Jo said to Cass when they were on the way back to her flat, not wanting to raise her hopes. 'But it's worth a try. Could I keep the notebook, by the way?'

Cass looked doubtful. 'Well, no, not really. I know I won't get my job back but if this little item will help me get even with NCB—' she patted the side of her bag with a vengeful smile — 'I'm going to hold on to it. After all, it's a lot more important to me than it is to you.'

Jo reluctantly gave up. Before she left, she had to broach something else to Cass, which might complicate her life still further. 'Have you ever been to Coventry?' she asked.

'No. Why?'

'That's where Sean was killed,' Jo said.

'In Coventry?' She sounded surprised.

'Well, on the outskirts. In a little wood near a pub and a reservoir.'

'The pub doesn't surprise me, but the rest of it does.' Cass frowned. 'What was he doing there?'

Jo sighed. Clearly Cass was not going to throw any light on this persistent question. But Jo felt she had to warn her that if the police ever heard her story, she would be a major suspect. Jo tried to explain this but the other woman seemed unconcerned. She didn't think the police would link her with Sean. 'Who knows except you?' she pointed out. 'Some people at the bank knew about Sean and me, but it's old news now — especially as I've left. People move on fast, don't they? No one but Vaz has my new address and I think I can trust him.'

'If the police do find you, the first thing they'll ask is what you were doing on the eighteenth of June,' Jo said. 'Oh, and do you have a car?'

'Never owned a car. No idea what I was doing on that day,' Cass answered. She gave it a bit more thought due to Jo's prompting but still could not remember much. 'I was here in London looking for a job, I think.'

'Well, if you remember the names of anyone you met that day, you might find they come in handy,' Jo advised. And that was how they left it.

Jo would not have been so relaxed in Cass's position. She didn't think the police would swallow Cass's story as readily as she had. It wasn't until she was on the Tube, heading towards Putney, that her suspicious nature reasserted itself and she began to wonder why she had.

CHAPTER FOURTEEN

Jo could have spent another useful half hour with Cass, trying to find out more about Sean, but Connor had called her that morning and invited her to dinner with his family.

'You said you wanted me to get you an interview with my mother,' Connor had reminded her. 'I've done better than that. You can meet the whole crew tonight and I've told them they have to answer your questions. The only drawback is, you have to accompany me.'

Truth be told, that wasn't much of a drawback, Jo had thought to herself guiltily. Succumbing to Connor's charm was a mistake from a professional point of view — and from a personal one. She still didn't trust him but of course she had agreed to go, knowing it was a golden opportunity.

'Quite right,' Macy said when she called him to tell him her plans for a change. 'You don't pass up chances like that. You go and see if you can find any skeletons lurking in the family cupboards.'

Macy would probably encourage her to sleep with Connor if he thought it would further the case, Jo thought cynically as she turned into the road where Connor lived. She had timed it about right. He was just getting out of his car as she came up to his house. The way he glanced up and down the street as he locked his car made him look almost furtive but then he saw her and his expression changed. 'How are the mean streets, Jo? And how is the weary gumshoe?' He seemed genuinely pleased to see her.

She grinned back at him. 'Well, it's the mean streets of Richmond upon Thames for me this evening, anyway.'

'I can promise you a decent dinner, if nothing else.' Connor held the front door open for her and followed her in, dumping his car keys, briefcase and jacket at strategic points on his way to the kitchen. 'Come in and have a drink to set you up for it.'

'How has your family taken Sean's death? Wouldn't it be better if I didn't butt in? I'm sure your mother doesn't want me around.'

'Probably not,' Connor agreed. He gathered up the breakfast dishes and deposited them in the sink. 'But here you are. They've not taken it too badly, I suppose. Or maybe it just hasn't sunk in yet.' He looked up from under a stray lock of hair and Jo noticed he seemed pale and stressed. 'It's getting to me though,' he admitted, 'especially after the gruelling hours the police put me through.'

Jo leaned on the kitchen worktop, watching while he rinsed and dried two glasses. 'I met someone interesting this afternoon,' she remarked. 'One of Sean's girlfriends. Cass. Do you know her?'

'Yes, she was an ex, you're right,' he answered. 'They were quite serious by Sean's standards. They must have been together at least three months.'

'Why didn't you mention her before? She said she used to stay here overnight so you must have met her.'

'Well, yes.' Connor shrugged and reached for a new bottle of Tanqueray from a kitchen cupboard. 'But they split up and I haven't heard him talk about her for months. She had left the bank so it was well and truly over.'

'But didn't you think of contacting her when Sean went missing?'

'No. Well, yes, I did think of it,' Connor answered, 'but I ruled it out. Unless I was going to hunt out all Sean's old girlfriends, there didn't seem much point.'

As always with Connor, Jo didn't know whether to believe him or not. He passed her a glass of gin and tonic with lots of ice.

'Coke?' he offered and for half a second, Jo thought he was going to top up her drink. Then she looked up and saw him delicately lining the powder up on a place mat. He took a straw out of a drawer and put it to his nose, pressed one nostril with long fingers and inhaled. 'I need this to be able to face my mother's dinner parties.'

Jo's doubts about Connor redoubled. She shook her head. 'Not for me. I'll settle for some booze and my best efforts with make-up. Is there anywhere I can get changed?'

Connor, not yet noticeably affected by either the drink or the cocaine, was obliging as ever. He showed her to Sean's bedroom. It looked tidier and Jo remarked on this.

'Oh yes. That was the police. They were here all day Saturday. Took a load of stuff away with them including the laptop and said they would come back for more. Of course, they don't explain what they're doing. I'm off to shower now, just come down when you're ready.'

Before getting changed, Jo had another look round the bedroom. Sifting through the papers now in neat piles on his desk, she came across the bank statement which showed the cash withdrawal from the Coventry bank on 18 June. She looked back to around the time Cass had been sacked and saw a cash withdrawal for £120, the amount she said had been planted in her make-up bag. It certainly supported Cass's story and Jo slipped it into the pocket of her holdall.

She took out the dark blue vest dress she had brought with her and examined it for creases. It had travelled well but somehow she felt that no matter how hard she tried to look her best she was not going to feel at her ease.

This instinct turned out to be true. If she had remembered Mrs Fitzpatrick as being elegant, she had underestimated her.

The woman was a beauty. Her pale hair was piled on her head, her earrings glinted discreetly and she looked sinuously thin in a pearl-grey silk suit, which made Jo feel brash in comparison. She looked drawn but greeted Jo with a gracious smile. She gave Connor a light hug but held on a moment longer than he did. 'I'm sorry,' she said weakly, her head turned away, 'I'd never noticed before how much alike you and Sean were.'

Connor looked desperate. 'Come on, don't cry now, and we can't leave Jo on the doorstep.'

'I'm sorry about Sean,' Jo said awkwardly.

Fiona Fitzpatrick accepted Connor's handkerchief and dabbed at her eyes. She turned to Jo. 'Oh yes, we've met, haven't we? Hello.' She extended her delicate long fingers. 'I do hope you're not going to ask us hundreds of tedious questions about poor Sean. I don't think I'm up to it.'

'I'll try not to,' Jo murmured. You needed all the sensitivity of a rhinoceros to be a good PI. She was obviously developing this quality because she followed them dutifully into the house.

'It's such a warm evening, we're on the lawn at present,' Fiona said, seemingly recovered. 'I'd love to dine outdoors but Connor's father thinks it's uncomfortable so we'll eat in the orangery as a compromise.'

It was hard to imagine Fiona Fitzpatrick as anyone's mother but Jo noticed that she took a maternal interest in Connor. While her polite chatter was directed at Jo, her eyes looked him over and she swept him off to help with the drinks as soon as she had introduced Jo to the other guests — 'Just the family,' as she put it.

In the cab on the way over, Connor had described them all so Jo could easily identify them before she was introduced. 'The miserable old bugger who moans about everything from the M25 to the price of fresh salmon is my father. My elder brother Kieran tries to be exactly like him, and his wife Gina will be tottering around on her high heels making comments about the weather.'

In fact Connor's father, Gerrard, was in the middle of a diatribe about the deficiencies of the education system but he broke off to shake hands with Jo. 'How do you come to know Connor? Through business, is it?' He could, unlike his wife, be described as middle-aged. He was dark and thickset, with little resemblance to Connor apart from something about the set of the shoulders and Connor's lively expression.

'Yes, business,' Jo said. 'I'm a private investigator. Connor is employing my firm.'

'Oh yes, you're that one, are you? Connor said something about you.' Gerrard Fitzpatrick regarded her for a moment and then looked out over the lawn. 'Can't the police be relied upon for that sort of work? Or is Connor just being unconventional as usual?'

'He doesn't strike me as particularly unconventional,' Jo remarked, but Gerrard began speaking over her reply.

'Remarkable how well Connor is doing, you know. Only just over thirty and he's already a partner. We're very pleased with him.'

Jo couldn't work out whether this was meant as information for her benefit or to warn her that Connor was out of her league. 'He and Sean were close,' Gerrard went on, frowning at her. 'It's been a great shock to us all.' Before she could respond, Connor and his mother came back with the drinks.

'Gerrard, have you been dominating our guest? Haven't you let her talk to the others yet? Come with me, Jo.' Fiona placed a glass of pale cold sherry in Jo's hand and introduced her to the couple on the terrace, who, Jo had noticed, were sitting in silence.

'Nice to meet you,' Kieran said. With his dull sports jacket and bored eyes, Jo decided he was distinctly less charming than Connor. His wife, who looked out of place in white silk dungarees and high heels, said a quick hello and then sat back, sipping a long drink.

'Jo is my private investigator.' Connor pulled up heavy wrought iron seats for himself and Jo.

‘Are you making so much money you need a minder now?’ Kieran responded. He had a leisurely way of speaking that took any sting out of this remark.

‘I’m trying to find out some more information about your brother, Sean,’ Jo said. ‘Can you tell me anything about him?’ When this brought no response, she added, ‘For instance, do you know who might have wanted to kill him?’

‘He had friends in low places,’ Kieran said. ‘I’ve put his death down to the company he kept.’

‘What sort of people?’

Kieran frowned at her. ‘Well, I don’t know them, for God’s sake. I had very little to do with Sean and the family had pretty well washed their hands of him.’

‘Except for Connor,’ Jo put in, catching Connor’s eye.

‘Well, I’ve said I didn’t know what he was up to half the time,’ Connor sounded embarrassed and a little awkward silence fell.

Jo took a sip of the excellent sherry and asked with slight sarcasm if they could think of anything else helpful.

As the two men said nothing, Gina looked at Jo earnestly. ‘Well, he was very good with figures,’ she said. While Jo wondered how to respond to this, Gina put down her phone and leaned over towards her. ‘What are you wearing to the funeral? Do you think it’s over the top to wear a veil? I’m not a blood relative, you see.’

‘I would think it would be all right,’ Jo said, aware that the two men had started talking to their father. Remarks about golf shots reached her ears while Gina confided in Jo her problems over choosing a suitable outfit.

‘I don’t look very good in black, do you? I’m a natural redhead and it tends to make me look washed out,’ Gina was saying when they were ushered in towards the table.

‘I don’t think people worry about that too much at a funeral. Black is probably safest,’ Jo heard herself say as she went into the orangery at Gina’s side. She almost clutched her head in despair. This was not going to get her anywhere.

The food was light and varied but the conversation didn't match. Gerrard and Kieran were both doctors and most of their conversation turned on hospital politics. Fiona's comments were limited to accommodating remarks or occasionally, like a good hostess, to encouraging the quieter ones to join in.

Jo had been surprised by Fiona's emotional scene on the doorstep but it seemed positively unreal that throughout the meal Sean's name was not mentioned once. She couldn't let them get away with this lightly. She didn't bother being subtle — if she waited for an opportunity, one might never arise. She made the most of a lull in the conversation. 'Does anyone have any idea why Sean would have gone to Coventry?'

Fiona Fitzpatrick was the first to recover. 'I've really no idea. Maybe you are best placed to say, Jo? What does Coventry have to recommend it?'

'Well, I don't think he went to visit the cathedral.' Jo looked round at the family, who all looked uneasy. 'I'm sorry to press this. But I have to try to find out what I can.'

'We've no connections with the place,' Gerrard responded, 'as I've told the police countless times. Sean was his very much his own man.'

'Oh, yes, we had the West Midlands Police tramping all over the carpets the whole weekend.' Fiona's gaze swept round the table. 'And I found something out about policemen. They all take three sugars in their tea. To a man. Isn't that interesting?'

There was a polite laugh. Jo sighed and helped herself to more salad. She knew Sean had been the younger son of three and one thing that occurred to her, as she let the salmon mousse linger on her tongue, was that in this family circle of consultants and stockbrokers, a middle manager of a bank would not shine bright.

After the meal, they moved to a comfortable room indoors and Gerrard produced the whisky decanter. Connor, accepting a second glass readily, became more loquacious and she heard him advising his father about what car he should buy. While Jo was wondering about her chances of persuading him to call a taxi soon, Fiona came up to her, preceded slightly by her perfume.

'How are your investigations going?' she asked in the same reserved, civil tones Jo had been hearing all evening.

'I'm making slow progress.'

'I just wanted a little word.' Fiona lowered her voice. 'You know we care deeply about Sean.' She put her head on one side with a serious expression and Jo noticed that her eye liner was still near perfect. She murmured something suitable in reply.

'It's just that Connor's too young and idealistic to see it, but we don't want a lot of fuss made. Of course we want to know what happened to Sean, but I've every faith in the police, so why don't you let Connor have a nil return?'

The conspiratorial note in her voice annoyed Jo. 'That wouldn't be very professional of me, would it?'

'Dear me, I hadn't realised private investigators thought of themselves as having a profession.' Fiona gave a trill of laughter.

'I have to do the job I am paid for,' she said. Out of the corner of her eye she could see Fiona's husband bearing down on them.

'Are you getting tired, darling?' he asked his wife. 'We shouldn't be up too late, not with tomorrow on the horizon.' Jo didn't entirely understand this but she was more than ready to leave. Fiona was staring back at her coldly. Jo got up without speaking and went to find Connor.

He was pouring himself another whisky and when he looked up at Jo, his eyes were distinctly unclear. She told him tersely that she was going home and would be in touch about the case. Connor insisted in his usual easy manner that she mustn't go without him. He put down his glass and went out to call a cab for both of them. Jo's anger had died down and left her with an intense feeling of boredom. She hesitated a moment, then followed Connor into the hall.

It seemed the little party was breaking up anyway. Kieran and Gina followed her out. Kieran was talking over his shoulder to his father. Gerrard Fitzpatrick apparently wanted to show his son some new security lights he had bought for the garage doors.

'Wait there. I won't be a minute,' Kieran said to his wife before he went after his father.

Gina folded her arms across the bib of her dungarees and leaned against the staircase. 'How boring,' she said to Jo.

'It doesn't sound like you're missing anything exciting,' Jo agreed, looking round for Connor.

Gina gave an unexpected giggle. 'I know that,' she said. 'Exciting is not the word for anything that happens in this house.' She had a soft face, her features indistinct apart from her small mouth.

'How do you put up with this supercilious bunch of hypocrites?' Jo wondered aloud.

'You don't mean that about Connor, surely?' Gina grinned. 'He's the spoilt baby of the family. He can do no wrong.'

'Not like Sean,' Jo commented. 'No one's got a good word to say about him.'

'He was the black sheep. Not as clever as the others — or even as nice-looking. I think he misbehaved just to draw attention to himself, like kids do.'

'People keep saying things like that, but what did he actually do?'

Gina dropped her voice to a whisper. 'There was the drugs and gambling and his marriage. His wife ended up hating him. I never blamed her for leaving like she did.'

'Who was she? What happened to her?'

'Valerie? Left the country, I believe. He met her at the bank. She had nobody but him and she worshipped him.'

'Do you have to leave now, Jo?' Fiona's distinct voice cut across them. 'Connor tells me he's called a cab.'

'Yes. Thank you for the lovely meal and for bringing yourself to be so polite to me,' Jo answered. Gina took a step away from Jo, as though not wanting to be associated with such daring. Connor, who appeared from behind his mother, seemed unabashed. He regarded Jo with wide-eyed amusement.

Fiona regained her poise after only a second — but Jo enjoyed that moment. The doorbell gave a muted ring and Connor weaved through the edgy little group of women to answer it. 'Cab's here,' he announced.

He held the door for Jo and they walked down the drive.

'You shoot from the hip, don't you?' he remarked. Jo was quite surprised when he got in the cab with her. She wouldn't have cared one way or the other but she saw him grinning at her and started to laugh.

The whole evening suddenly seemed hilarious. She recounted her conversation with Gina about what to wear at the funeral and they both roared hysterically. Recovering first, Jo called out to the taxi driver to take her to Connor's address, adding that she would go on to Euston Station.

'No,' Connor protested, 'you must stay with me tonight. I've got a very good sofa bed. Or you can have my bed — with or without me in it.'

'No, I want to get home,' Jo said. But Connor went on persuading her, promising her the sofa bed and complete privacy, and eventually she gave in. The amount Connor had imbibed, she didn't think he would be capable of anything remotely sexual and she believed him when he said he would not try.

'What was Sean's wife like? Why did they get divorced?' Jo demanded of Connor, who was slumped in one corner of the cab, still giving the occasional giggle. 'Could she have borne him a serious grudge?'

'Valerie?' Connor focused his eyes on her with obvious difficulty. 'Shouldn't think so. She was a bit of a drip. I told you he used to beat her about a bit, didn't I?'

'Not exactly, no.' This was the second time this evening that Connor had shocked her and she was glad it was dark in the cab so he didn't have the satisfaction of knowing. 'Is that why she left him?'

'I should think so.' Connor roused himself to look out of the cab window just as they turned into his street.

'And her name was definitely Valerie — not Rosie?' Jo suggested.

'Shit!' Connor dived down to the floor of the cab. 'Don't stop,' he said urgently to the driver. 'Keep going.'

'What's wrong?' Jo asked. 'Are you OK?'

The driver swore and demanded to know where he was supposed to go.

'Anywhere — just quickly. For Christ's sake, don't stop!' Connor shouted, still crouched on the floor of the cab. He tried to pull Jo down with him but she stared out of the window as the cab drove past the house. Two men were sitting on the garden wall looking around them. As the cab went past, one of them stood up and stared at it.

'Who are they?' Jo asked, turning her head to watch them as the cab passed.

'Where the bloody hell am I going?' the taxi driver grumbled.

Connor got up gingerly. 'A hotel—' he muttered. Jo thought she had never seen anyone sober up so fast. His face was white and his eyes terrified.

'Whereabloodybouts?' the taxi driver demanded. Connor named a hotel in Bayswater. He licked his lips and held his throat as if desperately thirsty.

'What was all that about?' Jo asked.

'I'll tell you when we get indoors,' Connor answered, his voice faint. Jo desisted. She decided she had better let him get over the shock. Predictably, his first question at the hotel was to find out how he could get a drink. He ordered a bottle to be brought up to his room. He booked two, one room for himself and one for Jo, but she followed him into his. She had no intention of staying there but she wanted an explanation before finding her own bed.

Connor slumped on the side of the bed. His hair hung over his bloodshot eyes and his tie knot lay limply on his chest. There was a knock at the door and the bottle of whisky arrived. Against Jo's better judgement, she poured some for him. Connor drank it and refilled it himself.

Jo sat down on a chair on the opposite side of the room. She was feeling a bit shocked herself. She had never seen a change come over anyone as suddenly as this. She knew it was the effect of the coke and drink as much as anything else but she still felt oddly disillusioned. He looked at her and took another drink.

'Who were those men?' Jo asked calmly.

'Sean's creditors. They're after me for money,' Connor said.

'Much money?'

'Thousands — more than I can lay my hands on right now but I am trying.'

'Why pay? Why not just tell the police?' Jo knew it couldn't be as simple as that. She sat and waited. Connor put down the glass and said nothing. 'Is this something to do with your supply of coke?'

Connor nodded. 'Sean was the dealer. I just bought some off him and now and again gave a little bit out to friends.'

'For money?'

'God, yes — that stuff is too expensive to just give away.'

'So you dealt too.' On one level, Jo found it hard to believe she was having this conversation. She knew nothing much about drugs. She had only ever smoked a bit of dope in her life. Half an hour ago she had even contemplated sleeping with this man.

'Just to friends,' Connor was saying. 'Sean got hold of the stuff. Trouble is, he died owing money to his supplier. Don't ask me how, I don't know. Or maybe they're even lying about him owing them but it doesn't matter much because they're coming after me for it. I'm going to get it. I just need a few more days.'

'Why didn't you tell me about all this before? They could have had something to do with Sean's death.'

'Wouldn't make sense if he owed them money.' Connor sighed. 'I guessed it might have to come out but I wanted to avoid it if I could.' He gave Jo a wry look. 'This kind of thing wouldn't go down well at work. Don't go broadcasting it.'

'Who are these people? The men who were sitting on your garden wall?'

Connor threw up his arms. 'I honestly don't know. The guy who rings me never gives a name. I know Sean used to meet someone in a club to get his supplies.'

'Which club?'

It was a little while before Connor answered and then she had to strain to hear. 'I don't even know which club. I didn't want to get too involved.' He gave Jo an ironic smile.

'How often have these men been in touch with you? Have you seen them before?'

'Never. Never before.' He refilled his glass, spilling some whisky onto his hand. 'It's the funeral tomorrow, you know. Are you going to be there?' He tilted backwards as he spoke, sliding into a prone position while still holding his glass upright.

'More to the point, are you?' Jo sighed, watching his eyes close. It seemed she was not going to get much more information out of him tonight. She told him she was going to bed.

'I'm fine. Don't worry about me,' he called as she let the door close softly behind her.

Lying on the bed in her hotel room and listening to the noise of the traffic outside, Jo wasn't sure whether she wanted to carry on with this case. Any sympathy for Sean Fitzpatrick or his brother had evaporated.

After ten minutes, she got up, went to the bathroom and vomited up her dinner.

CHAPTER FIFTEEN

Jo was in the same uncharacteristically depressed state of mind when she woke up the next morning. It took her a minute or so to realise there was someone knocking at the door and another minute to orientate herself sufficiently to open it. A man in hotel uniform stood in the corridor holding a pot of coffee and a plate of croissants, which she hadn't ordered.

She fumbled for her watch. 'Thanks, but—'

'Mr Fitzpatrick sent these and says he'll pop in to see you in half an hour,' the waiter told her. 'It's twenty past nine,' he added.

Jo poured herself a coffee and manoeuvred her heavy limbs to the window. Outside the traffic roared down Bayswater Road and it was raining. 'Good day for a funeral,' she murmured. After her second coffee she stood in the shower for a long time and then dressed quickly, aware that Connor would be knocking on the door any minute.

Her head ached but a vague sense of duty prompted her to ring Vaz at the bank. She dialled his number while sitting on the edge of the bed taking disconsolate bites of a croissant.

'Hello, I thought you'd call,' Vaz said.

Jo came straight to the point. She was not in the mood for pleasantries. 'Did you get anywhere with checking those account numbers?'

'Yes, nothing special about them. They were all closed accounts.'

'Oh. Who did they belong to? Sean?'

'No. Various people, no connections between them that I could see,' Vaz said in a near whisper. 'Why are you asking me to do this?'

'I'm concerned about Cass. Look, I know you can't speak freely but did you recognise any of the people these accounts belonged to? Were they all different?'

'Yes, all different. No, none I knew,' Vaz said. 'How is she, is she OK?'

'Cass? Not particularly.' Jo sighed. 'Oh well, thanks for trying.'

'One thing,' Vaz added. 'They had all been closed recently.'

'Recently? Before the eighteenth of June, though?'

'That's right. All closed in the month prior to that date. I have to go now.'

'Can you keep looking for something? I'm sure Sean closed all those accounts because Cass found out they existed. She doesn't know any more but there must have been something funny going on. Thanks, Vaz.' Jo put her fingers on her forehead and found she could pinpoint the ache. It was unfair to feel so bad when she hadn't even drunk all that much, she thought.

Then Connor knocked at the door and she felt worse. To her surprise, he looked his usual neat self.

'Sleep well?' he asked.

'Not really,' Jo said.

'Me neither.' He gave her a rueful smile. 'I have to go back to Putney. Sean's funeral is in Richmond, St Thomas's at twelve o'clock. I'll settle up for us here and maybe see you . . . ?' The question trailed off. He gave her a quick look and added, 'Or maybe not.'

'Either Macy or I will be in touch,' Jo said, remembering that this man was paying her wages.

'OK. Listen, I'm sorry about last night. I'm not going to make excuses but—'

Jo cut him short, saying she had to catch a train to Coventry. They walked down the corridor together, Connor chatting genially as usual and Jo beginning to feel slightly more kindly towards him, so that they managed to part on reasonable terms. She was glad to be left on her own again, though, to set off for Euston and home.

At the station she found that all trains bound for the Midlands were suffering delays due to vandalism on the track. She groaned aloud. For a while she couldn't think of anything else to do except stand around with all the other people, craning her neck to reread the notice. It occurred to her that she should call Macy. He had probably been expecting her to let him know how she had got on at the bank yesterday. She tried his mobile without any luck so she called the office and soon found herself listening to Celia's indomitably cheerful tones.

'Thank goodness you've phoned, Jo. We've been wondering where you were. Mr Macy was ringing your flat last night and he even called round this morning in case your phone was out of order.'

'I suppose he expected me to report back.' Another thing that had gone wrong, Jo thought glumly.

'Well, yes, and I think he was a bit worried about you. Are you all right?'

'Mm, sort of — I suppose I ought to tell him the latest developments. You'd better put me through.'

'Oh, he's not here now. He's gone to Sean Fitzpatrick's funeral. He asked if you could meet him there if you called. Do you know where it is?'

Jo admitted, somewhat reluctantly, that she did. She didn't want to go anywhere but home. She certainly didn't want to go to a funeral. On the other hand, the journey home by train was obviously going to be slow. She found out from Celia that Macy had brought his car so she would be able to get a lift back to Coventry. She need not encounter any of the Fitzpatricks, she reasoned, and in any case she would probably be too late for the funeral. She hoped Macy would still be around. She told Celia she would meet him there.

Jo's day seemed to be improving. The rain had stopped before she reached Richmond. As she walked up the hill, she saw Macy leaning against the churchyard wall. His shoulders were hunched, the collar of his dark jacket was turned up and despite his suit and tie he managed to look thoroughly out of place and suspicious.

'You'll give private investigators a bad name,' Jo advised.

'Oh, you've turned up at last, have you? You've missed the funeral. They all packed off to the wake about five minutes ago.'

'Can't say I'm sorry.'

'Come on, let's go for a drink.' Macy looked at her face and frowned. 'You look terrible.' He led the way to a dark little pub on Richmond Hill, which was almost entirely empty at that time of day.

'You haven't got a paracetamol, have you?' Jo guessed it was the kind of thing Macy would have about his person. She was right. He bought her a chilled bottle of mineral water and handed her two painkillers. Jo, absurdly, felt tears come into her eyes at this little kindness. *God, I must be in a worse state than I thought*, she thought and swallowed the tablets.

'So where did you get to last night?' Macy asked.

'A hotel in Bayswater Road with Connor Fitzpatrick,' Jo said and saw with some gratification that Macy's gaze became unusually focused. She told him about yesterday's events without going into details. He didn't ask many questions and kept glancing at the door when anyone came in. 'Are you expecting someone?' Jo interrupted herself to ask.

'Yes. Nick Walmsley, Sean's boss. I spoke to him after the funeral. He said he would just show his face at the Fitzpatricks' house and would come down here for a drink.'

‘Why do you want to speak to him?’

‘I don’t, particularly. He was the only person there who didn’t totally ignore me,’ Macy admitted.

‘That figures.’ Jo laughed. ‘He’ll be surprised to see me. He was interviewing me for a job yesterday.’ She did not have time to finish her report to Macy before Nick’s smart-suited figure appeared at their table.

‘Hi — dreadful occasions, aren’t they, funerals? Can I get . . .’ He paused as his eyes met Jo’s. ‘Didn’t I see you yesterday?’ As realisation dawned, a palpably insincere smile crossed his face. ‘So you weren’t a real candidate, then? Well, that’s a good one. I suppose you have to be up to all sorts of tricks in your line of work. It’s fortunate I didn’t give you the job,’ he added.

‘It’s all right, I wouldn’t have accepted.’ She played along with the joke, but behind his good-humoured expression, she detected a malicious edge.

Nick laughed. ‘Let me get you both a drink anyway.’

Jo finished her story while Nick was at the bar. ‘So Connor and Sean were into coke and Connor has to find the money to pay off Sean’s suppliers. And I think Sean was involved in some sort of scam at the bank too.’

Macy looked exasperatingly vague but Jo guessed he had taken it all in. He got up to give Nick a hand with the drinks. ‘It’s good of you to come,’ he said as they both took their places around the small table. ‘I need to find out as much as I can about Sean.’

‘You don’t want to trouble the family at a time like this,’ Nick agreed. He took a sip of his beer. ‘I’m quite happy to help if it takes some of the pressure off them. I’ve known Sean years so I can probably tell you anything you want to know.’ He focused on Macy and hardly seemed to notice Jo, who was pouring out her second glass of water. She found it harder to trust his open-eyed expression since her conversation with Cass.

‘You’ve known him years, you say?’ Macy sipped his drink.

'We worked together in London, our first jobs and both of us looking up from the bottom of the greasy pole. So we were friends then and stayed in touch afterwards. I was working at the bank when Sean was looking for a job. His IT business failed so I suggested the bank and he got the job. I don't think he realised he would end up working for me, though.' He chuckled. 'That must have been a bit hard for him to take — as he was always supposed to be the brilliant one. That's often how it goes, though, isn't it? These bright sparks burn themselves out.' He hesitated, perhaps realising that what he had said was too apt.

'You were close friends, then?' Macy asked before Nick could recover.

'Yes — as far as work allowed. Unlike Sean, I've got my career and a wife to think about so I couldn't always be at his beck and call, out on the town every night — you know the sort of thing.'

'I suppose you had to see the police and they took a statement?' Macy said lazily, his eyes wandering around the bar.

'Not just from me but from virtually everyone at work. And they even went to see my wife too, which I thought was a bit of a cheek.'

'Mm. So what did you say? In your statement, I mean?'

'All they were really interested in was where I was the night Sean died.' Nick sat back in his chair and massaged his neck. 'I was working late — not alone, fortunately for me.'

'Oh yes, with Carol, your PA?' Jo chipped in.

'That's right.'

'She told me.' Jo thought this conversation was getting too cosy so she decided to take a hand. 'I also met Cass Baxter yesterday,' she put in with a smile.

'Oh dear.' Nick sighed. 'You do know she's got a chip on her shoulder the size of the Shard, don't you?' He shot Macy a conspiratorial glance as if to recruit his sympathy. Macy, who was in saintly mode today, did not give him any encouragement, Jo noticed.

'Cass reckons Sean got her the sack and you might have known something about this,' she said. She had decided on a direct accusation so she could watch Nick's reaction.

He shook his head on an intake of breath as if in sympathy. 'I know, I know. She's been to me with this story. But as I said to her, if she's got that good a case, she should take us to an employment tribunal. She didn't seem too keen on that for some reason.' This was said with another smug glance in Macy's direction.

Macy buried his face in his pint glass. He left it to Jo to continue this line of questioning, although he must have wondered what she was on about as she had not had time to explain about Cass.

'She might have a better case than you think,' she said. Having decided to take the bull by the horns, there was no point in holding back now. 'You know about Sean's little notebook? It has some very interesting numbers in it . . .' Jo let this sentence tail off and watched him.

Nick raised his sandy eyebrows. 'Ms Baxter has really led you up the garden path, hasn't she? Why should I be interested in a list of Sean's old girlfriends? I'm happily married.' He gave another little laugh. But Jo noticed he was drinking faster. Most people slowed down towards the end of a pint.

'So as far as you know, Sean wasn't up to anything dubious at the office?' Jo asked.

'No. We had the auditors in only a couple of months ago — they went away perfectly happy, so you don't just have to take my word for it.'

'And you would know?' Macy put in. 'I mean, if he was up to something, you would know — as his boss.'

'Of course. I can save you some time here,' Nick said. 'You are going down a blind alley with this one. Sean may not have been totally respectable in some ways, but as far as the bank is concerned, he is as clean as a whistle.' Nick downed the last of his drink and set his glass down. 'Speaking of the bank, I must be getting back to it. I hope I've been some help.' He got to his feet, holding out a hand to Macy and then to Jo with only a shade of reluctance. They watched him leave, his movements lithe and comfortable as if he had already forgotten them before he reached the pub door. Macy looked at Jo and for once she knew exactly what he was thinking.

'Nick is involved, isn't he?'

'In shit up to his ears,' Macy said. 'And the clever thing to do next is to check his alibi.'

CHAPTER SIXTEEN

'I've already spoken to his PA, Carol. She says she was with him until quarter past eight that Friday night so he probably couldn't have got to Coventry in time,' Jo said.

'That's assuming the time of Sean's death ties in with the broken down Vauxhall in the lay-by and the blonde girl and so on but what if that is totally spurious?' Macy leaned across the table towards her. He had suddenly taken on one of his rare, animated moods and Jo wondered if the moon had just changed signs. 'Say he died later,' Macy went on, 'then Nick could have got there.'

'How would Nick know where he was?'

'A minor point.' Macy dismissed it with a sweeping gesture which almost knocked over Jo's water bottle. 'The post-mortem was yesterday afternoon so the police should have a better idea of the time of death by now. And we want to know where Nick went after he left the office. I'll call Anita.'

While Macy called DS Anwar, Jo went to the ladies, approaching the mirror cautiously to see if she looked any better. She didn't. However, she reassured herself that she didn't look any worse either and a touch-up with make-up helped a bit. When she returned to the table, Macy was his usual gloomy self. 'They've placed the time of death at between nine and ten p.m. Nick left the office at eight o'clock, so it looks like he's in the clear.'

'I'm not convinced. Any other news?'

'Anita says they've unearthed a few more witnesses who saw Sean on Friday the eighteenth. The last sighting was in the Castaway at about half past eight. And they've found his car. It was in one of the car parks at Heathrow Airport. No unusual prints but they're doing a thorough search now.'

'Did you find out where Nick went after work on Friday?'

'Yes. All very cosy and domesticated. He went home to his wife in St Albans. Mrs Walmsley supports his story but Anita has some doubts about her. Do you fancy a visit to wifey?'

'You mean your pal Anita gave you the address?'

'We did a swap. I told her what Alan's found out about the Vauxhall.'

'Well, that's more than I know,' Jo said peevishly.

'I forgot to say. Alan found a mechanic who remembers selling it only a few weeks ago to a young woman, who paid cash and gave her name as Norton. Apparently she was blonde.'

'Before we go off to meet Mrs Walmsley, I've got a call to make too.' Without explaining further, Jo went outside to ring Vaz, hoping he wouldn't be at lunch.

He didn't sound all that pleased to hear from her. 'I knew you'd be in touch again,' he said. 'Luckily this isn't a bad moment, as I'm on my own. You realise my career prospects could be as dismal as Cass's after this, don't you?'

'You mean you've found something?'

'I think so.' He dropped his voice so that Jo had to strain to hear him. 'But I need to get some more information this afternoon. Cass rang. She remembered certain files Sean didn't want the auditors to see. I'm going to try and find them and meet you both at Ponti's at half past six. Cass knows where it is.'

'You'd better tell me — I'll meet you both there.' Vaz explained and she noted down the details. 'If Cass calls again, tell her to hold on to that address book.'

'I think she will.' Vaz's voice became more formal. 'OK, thank you for calling. Goodbye.'

Macy was finishing off a plate of chips when Jo rejoined him. He offered her some but she couldn't face even one. Her headache had eased but her stomach still felt queasy.

'Tell me about Cass and this mysterious notebook on our way to the car,' Macy said. 'Why do you think it's so important?'

It was raining again outside and they walked briskly

'Because as soon as Sean knew Cass had got hold of the notebook, he closed all the accounts listed in the back and got her sacked,' Jo replied, slightly out of breath.

'Why didn't he just ask her to give the book back? Or somehow make her give it back? Wouldn't that have been simpler?'

Jo felt her damp hair, which she knew would be going hopelessly curly. 'Maybe getting the book back wouldn't have made any difference. Perhaps once Cass had seen it, Sean feared she would be able to work out for herself what he was up to — as she worked at the bank. That's why he had to get rid of her.'

'But we don't know what this scam was.' Macy got in the car and Jo waited in the rain while he leaned over and opened the passenger door.

'No, but Vaz — he works at the bank — is trying to find out. Cass was sure Nick helped Sean get her the sack, which could mean he's involved in the same business. Or maybe Sean forced Nick into helping — had some sort of hold over him, perhaps.' Jo paused, feeling quite pleased with this theory.

'Could be.' Macy jabbed a postcode into the satnav. 'Either way, it gives Nick Walmsley a wonderful reason for wanting Sean to disappear for ever. We're getting to the stage where we could hand this case over to the police entirely. They could do the donkey work then.'

* * *

The Walmsleys lived on a main road leading out of St Albans. The house was one of a line of uninspiring just-about-detached houses built on an embankment, with their front lawns sloping steeply down to the road. Jo was trying to read the numbers when Macy braked sharply. A car had stopped in front of him. Macy's old Ford finished inches from the back of the shiny pastel green Fiat. He was about to pull away, swearing, when Jo told him not to bother.

'This is it. Number ninety-six. We're here.' She stared up at the respectable, double-fronted 1950s house with its tidy, white-painted windows and gable.

Then she noticed the two women getting out of the green car in front. The shorter one in low heels and a pink trench coat looked familiar. Jo put her hand on Macy's arm. 'That's Carol, Nick's PA.'

Carol locked the car. 'Sorry,' she mouthed with a rueful grin, 'forgot to signal.' She waved her left arm in a rough approximation of a hand signal. The other woman, older and not dressed for rain, waited patiently on the pavement. She was holding house keys.

'That must be Nick's wife,' Jo said. 'What are these two doing together?'

'Shall we say hello?' Macy suggested, opening the car door.

Carol's smile became more anxious when she saw Macy get out. 'Sorry. My fault entirely,' she said. 'No damage done though—' She stopped when she saw Jo and for the second time that day, Jo enjoyed the dramatic effect she created simply by making an appearance.

'Oh, hello. We met at the bank yesterday,' Carol said, confused. 'What a coincidence.'

'Well, not really,' Jo explained. 'I wasn't a genuine candidate for the job. Actually, we're private investigators and we've come to see if we can have a quick word with Mrs Walmsley?'

'With me?' This came out almost as a squawk from the woman who had been standing watching. She was trying ineffectually to pull her summer blazer round her to keep off some of the rain.

Carol stared at them. 'Good grief. Well, you meet all sorts. I suggest we all go in out of the rain — if that's all right with you, Mrs Walmsley?'

'I suppose so.' The other woman shrugged and led the way up the path. Jo and Macy exchanged a quick amused glance and followed.

'I don't know what Nick's going to say about it all,' Mrs Walmsley said as they trooped down her hall.

'No, neither do I,' Carol muttered under her breath.

'It's all right,' Macy said, at his most reassuring, 'we've only just come from speaking to Nick and he knows that we're looking into Sean Fitzpatrick's death. I'm David Macy by the way—' he held out his hand — 'and this is Jo Hughes.'

'Lynne Walmsley.' The older woman's handshake was limp and brief, her worried eyes darting from one to the other. Her lipstick was smudged and her face was pale and doubtful under over-dyed brown hair.

'Carol Forrest,' the PA said, 'but we have sort of met.' She nodded briefly at Jo and then Macy. 'And now we've got the introductions out of the way, may I suggest a cup of tea? If you show me where the kitchen is, Mrs W, I'll make it while you go and sit down. And I think you were going to take a tablet, weren't you? Should I fetch one for you?'

'Oh, if you wouldn't mind,' Lynne said, as if she was used to being looked after. 'The kitchen's through there and the tablets are in the drawer nearest the door. I'd be so grateful.' She turned to Jo and Macy and gave a lacklustre smile. 'You'd better come and sit down, I suppose.'

She showed them into the front room, which was furnished in a conservative but comfortable style. She took off her damp blazer and sank down onto one of the armchairs.

Still slightly mystified but enjoying herself, Jo sat next to Macy on the sofa. 'Are you all right?' she asked as Lynne sat back and closed her eyes.

'Oh, yes, yes,' Lynne said without opening them, 'I've just had a very, very bad day. That's all. I don't know why I did it. It's a good job that woman has a heart after all.'

Carol entered the room during this speech but seemed unabashed. She tapped Lynne's arm and held out a tablet and a glass of water. Lynne accepted both wordlessly. 'Tea won't be long,' Carol said.

'I'll feel better in a minute.' Lynne smiled at Jo and Macy reassuringly, as if this must be their biggest concern.

Macy cleared his throat. 'Mrs Walmsley, I expect the police have spoken to you about where your husband was when Sean Fitzpatrick died.'

'Yes, a policewoman took a statement yesterday. I must admit I thought that would be the end of it. But I should have known.' She sighed and laid her head back, closing her eyes again. 'Nick, Nick, Nick. He's the bane of my existence. I don't know what's up with him. He's not sleeping. He's never here. I don't know what to do.' Lynne finished on a low wail and sat up, scrabbling for her handkerchief.

Carol came back just then, pushing the teapot, cups and saucers on an old-fashioned trolley. 'You're not upsetting yourself again, are you? Pour yourself a cup of tea, you'll feel better.'

Lynne looked at Carol over the tea things. 'You won't tell him, will you? It's just going to make things worse if he knows I went to the bank to see you.'

Carol poured herself some tea. 'I won't say a word,' she promised. 'We all make mistakes.'

'Why did you go to the bank?' Jo asked. She was prepared to be patient up to a point but she felt if she didn't ask some questions, these two odd women may draw a veil over whatever mystery they had uncovered and she would be no wiser.

'To find out what was going on.' Lynne sat back with her cup and saucer. 'I had to know what he was up to. But now I'm no wiser—' her face creased up again — 'I thought—'

'She thought Nick was having an affair with me,' Carol said with a little self-conscious laugh.

'You don't deny you cover up for him when I ring. You always say he's at meetings. Who has meetings at eight o'clock at night, I want to know?' Lynne said, her voice rising.

'We've been through this.' Carol handed out cups of tea to Jo and Macy, who were studiously avoiding looking at each other. 'I'll admit, I do tell porkies on his behalf. It's part of a PA's job to cover up for her boss. But I don't always know where he goes.'

'You mean he goes out of the office? These nights when you're working late?' Jo asked.

Carol looked down and made a little moue with her lips. 'Well, yes. Now and again. I told you I do half his work, didn't I?'

'But, Carol, you may be covering up for something really important—'

Lynne suddenly banged her cup down. 'But who is he having an affair with? I know there's someone. I've found her clothes in a suitcase. I know he's going to leave me, I know—'

'What suitcase?' Macy asked. He succeeded in distracting her.

She brought her brimming eyes to his. 'He's got his lover's clothes in there,' she said.

'Show me.' Macy put down his cup and saucer and stood up. 'Come on.' He held out his arm.

Lynne took it and got to her feet. 'All right. Come with me. I'm not making it up, you know.'

Jo had been hoping for a quiet word with Carol but Lynne insisted that all four of them went with her. 'Carol, you need to see this too or you will never understand — or forgive me for thinking—'

'Nonsense, nothing to forgive,' Carol said, but she followed her boss's wife upstairs all the same.

The main bedroom was dominated by a large double bed covered by a white quilt and lace pillows. Lynne slid back one of the wardrobe doors and took out a cream leather suitcase.

'I found this locked in the boot of his car,' she said in low tones. 'He's not the only one who can't sleep. The difference is, I've never been a good sleeper. The other night I waited until he'd finally dropped off. I took his keys and searched his car. I knew if there was anything he didn't want me to see, that's where he'd keep it. I never go in his car, you see, unless I'm with him. I don't drive.' She placed the suitcase on the bed and took a key from a bedside drawer. 'I got this off his key ring. God help me when he finds out. He'll definitely leave me. I never realised I could be so devious.'

'So why did you suddenly become suspicious?' Jo asked.

'I told you. He's been acting oddly. Staying out even later than usual—' she shot a look at Carol, who was standing at the back — 'At work, he said.'

Lynne opened the suitcase, which was crammed with women's clothes. It was packed reasonably neatly but the very fact it was so full meant the top layer had become disordered. The lace of a camisole dripped over the side, some smoky grey knickers lay on top and below them, what looked like a lemon slip. The heavier fabric of a dress or coat could be seen underneath.

'He must be planning to run off with her.' Lynne gazed down at the clothes, her eyes shining with tears.

Jo looked over at Carol, who was peering at the contents of the case from a distance. Her face registered surprise and then two high spots of colour appeared on her cheeks.

Macy sifted through the layers of clothes. 'Can I unpack some of them?' he asked Lynne.

'Go ahead.' She sighed. 'I've been through it all. There's no name on anything. Nothing personal.'

Macy laid some of the clothes on the bed in neat piles and shook out a heavy jacket, which had been at the bottom. He held it up for Jo to see. It was well-made and in distinctive red-and-white leather.

'Well, I must get back to work,' Carol's practical voice came from behind them. 'If you're all right now, Mrs W?'

'I'll show you out,' Jo offered and followed Carol down the stairs. 'What's going on?' she hissed in Carol's ear. 'You know, don't you? Whose clothes are they? Not yours?'

They reached the hall and Carol headed for the front door. 'No. I've really no idea. He used to ask me to cover for him while he went out once a week. To meet someone — or a different lot of someones — I never asked.'

'But why lie for him? And to the police too?'

Carol opened the door and looked out at the steady rain. 'As I said, it's part of my job. Also his career is my career — at least partly — and he's doing well. When the police asked me, I automatically covered up for Nick. On Friday nights he always went out about six and I stayed on at work. It's just a coincidence that Sean happened to die on a Friday. Nick's been going out on Friday evenings for the last three years and the man wouldn't harm a fly. I know him.'

'But you don't know what he does on Friday nights,' Jo pointed out.

'It's none of my business. But I know he doesn't go swanning up the M1 to kill his best friend. For one thing, he always leaves his car at work and it was there that night too when I left.' Carol sighed. 'I can see it all seems odd to you, that I have such loyalty to my boss and to the bank. Especially when there's no sex involved. But I'm like that. I'd rather be at work than at home, to be honest. I'd rather be number crunching for that weekly report than half-dead of boredom in front of the telly. Nick's just a good boss and his Friday nights off are nothing to do with me.' Carol gathered her trench coat around her, gave Jo a last look and stepped out into the rain.

Jo watched her get into her car. Macy and Lynne came down the stairs. Macy was obviously preparing to leave, while the woman looked tired and depressed.

'Will you be all right?' Jo asked.

'I'm going to my mother's,' she said. 'I'll pack a bag so I can stay overnight. It's not far — just two stops on the Tube.'

'If you pack quickly, I'll give you a lift there,' Macy offered.

Lynne looked pleased and went back upstairs to get ready. Jo was relieved. The woman seemed so volatile, she would have worried about leaving her on her own, but she couldn't help a quick glance at her watch. She hoped she was going to get to Ponti's on time to meet Vaz and Cass.

* * *

They only just made it. Macy seemed to have invited himself along to the meeting with Vaz and by the time they had found somewhere to park in Stonebridge, there was little chance to argue. They had to hurry between late, straggling commuters. Even so, they were fifteen minutes late.

The café was almost empty. It was a dark, narrow place, which mainly catered to lunchtime trade. Jo bought two Americanos at the counter and recognised Vaz and Cass, heads close together over a small table.

Neither Cass nor Vaz noticed them until Jo was virtually at Cass's elbow. Jo apologised for being late and introduced Macy and the other two shifted along the bench seat so all four could squash around.

'So what could you find out from those account numbers?' Jo asked as soon as they were settled.

Vaz, still exquisitely smart but looking tired, was drinking a glass of milk. 'I'm afraid you're probably right about Sean.'

'Why? What was he doing?'

Vaz whipped up his milk with a straw. 'Those accounts. I've been looking at them all day in my spare minutes. At first I couldn't see it. The only odd thing about them was that they were all closed within a short time of each other. They all had fairly large sums going in and coming out on a daily basis. That's a bit unusual, but it wouldn't make an auditor raise his eyebrows.'

Vaz's eyes flickered back to Cass but he kept to the point. 'Then I tried to look for the files that Cass mentioned.

I could only find two — I didn't have all that much time to look — but the forms for opening the account were not recorded where they should be. I think Sean must have set them up without proper authorisation. That means they could be false accounts. Then I noticed that they were linked to real accounts.'

'What does that mean?' Jo asked.

'Linked accounts are like a current and deposit account belonging to the same person,' Cass put in. 'Or if someone is paying off a personal loan to another bank customer — like their mother or something — their accounts would be linked. It means money can be transferred from one to the other easily.'

Jo worked it out aloud. 'So Sean had made up false accounts and linked them to real ones so he could get money out of the real ones?'

'Yes, basically,' Vaz agreed. 'The clever way he did it was to take money from an account at the start of the day's business, put it in one of his false accounts, invest it on the stock market and return the money at the close of business. The customer lost a day's interest every time he did it but otherwise would be none the wiser.'

'Do you think Nick Walmsley knew about this?' Jo asked.

'Someone else must have helped him — Nick would be the obvious person because Nick would have had to cover up for him. Nick would have had to agree those new accounts being set up without full authorisation.' Vaz turned back to Cass. 'At least this might mean you get your job back. It's hard to believe it of Sean, though, isn't it? I thought he was just interested in having a good time.'

'How far was Nick involved, do you think?' Macy asked.

Vaz lifted his shoulders. 'Equally guilty, but I would guess Sean did the dirty work of switching the money from one account to another. Sean set up the system, I imagine, and from what I can see, he's been running it for at least two years. Nick would have had to turn a blind eye at the right moments and approve the transfer forms. And help keep the auditors at bay.'

'Actually, it's hard to see what was in it for Nick,' Cass said. 'He's well-known for being ambitious and this would bring his career to a full stop for—'

'Money,' Macy finished.

'Yes, but I bet Sean talked him into it,' Cass persevered, 'or maybe he could somehow have forced Nick to go along with the idea.'

'Once Nick found out what Sean was doing and didn't say anything, he would be just as implicated as Sean,' Vaz observed. 'That in a way would give Sean a hold over him. What do you want me to do with this information?'

'Whatever you think you should,' Jo advised. 'Tell your boss for a start, I suppose.'

'We're going to tell the police about it as soon as possible,' Macy said. 'Are you willing to give us the notebook, Cass? To show them.'

Cass handed it over a little reluctantly. Vaz looked at her with an admiring smile. 'It was Cass telling me about those files that finally completed the picture,' he said. 'I hope you get your job back. You ought to.'

'Doubt it,' she said. 'But at least they might be persuaded to give me a decent reference now. Thanks to you.'

Jo could see that her and Macy's presence was superfluous. She thanked Vaz for helping and made an excuse to leave. She and Macy went out into the stuffy evening air together.

CHAPTER SEVENTEEN

They walked back to Macy's car. The rain had stopped hours ago but the clouds remained and the air was stale and heavy with fumes.

'So who is Nick's lover?' Jo wondered aloud.

'Why not Carol?' Macy suggested. 'She told one lie about Nick's whereabouts. Why not a bigger lie?'

'I don't think so.' Jo shook her head, thinking of her conversation with Carol on the Walmsleys' doorstep. 'She convinced me, anyway. I think this is a triangular puzzle and we're only looking at two corners of it. We've got the partnership between Sean and Nick. Taurus and Scorpio. The materialistic bull was outwitted by the ambitious scorpion but there has to be someone else . . .'

'What are you rambling on about?' Macy unlocked the car.

'Nick is Scorpio. Lynne told me when I went to help her pack her overnight bag. Scorpio is the opposite sign to Taurus and for ruthlessness, they beat Taurus every time.'

Macy looked bemused. 'I don't know about you but I can't do all this work on an empty stomach.' He got into the car. 'Let's go and eat. I'll pay.'

'You don't have to pay—' Jo began. Someone had once told her that her determination not to be obliged to anyone amounted to an obsession. But it didn't stop her.

'See it as part of your expenses,' Macy interrupted. 'And I won't consult you about the restaurant, does that make you feel any better?'

Jo started to argue but gave up. She could see Macy wasn't listening anyway.

'More and more, I think this is out of our hands. Tomorrow I'm going to see Anita.' He was waiting to join traffic on the main road. 'There's only so much we should keep from the police and I think we're about to cross the line into their territory.'

'But we've probably crossed it already,' Jo argued. 'And what about Connor? What will we tell him?'

'What we know,' Macy said. 'We've earned our crust as far as he's concerned. He's not expecting us to make him a present of his brother's murderer trussed up and ready for justice. I've a good idea Nick Walmsley must have got rid of Sean, who had become a high-risk, unreliable maverick and knew too much about him.'

'We have no evidence. We know he had a good reason to. We don't know where he was between five o'clock and eleven that night. But we have nothing to tie him to the actual murder. His car was at the bank, too, don't forget.'

'Details. The police will sort them out. They ought to know all this stuff about the fraud Nick and Sean were running.'

'There's still an awful lot we don't know,' Jo maintained. Why did conversations with Macy usually make her irritable, she wondered? He was always overlooking important details when it suited him. She was sorry she had agreed to eat with him. In any case, she thought, as they passed a sign to the M4, he probably had a motorway service area in mind.

'All right,' he was saying, 'we know Nick Walmsley must have had something to do with this scam of Sean's.' He turned into a dusty side street and slowed down to pass a line of parked cars.

'Vaz seemed to think it was certain. If so, then why would Nick kill Sean? It wouldn't have been very sensible,' Jo pointed out. 'Goose and golden egg and all that.'

Macy's choice of restaurant was a Spanish one on the corner of a run-down residential street. There were plastic vine leaves and empty wine bottles strung up outside. To Jo, it looked the kind of place where the food had to be wonderful or it would never have kept going. She and Macy took the only empty table, which was squashed between the wall and a couple who were sitting gazing at each other in adoring silence.

'We know Nick lied to the police about his whereabouts on Friday night,' Macy went on. 'I can't see why you're coming to his defence now.'

'I'm not and I'm sure you're right about Sean being a maverick who couldn't be trusted. I get all that. It's just that we're missing something obvious.' Jo stared at the laminated menu without reading it. To ignore important details would offend any Virgo and Jo was determined to work out whatever it was they had overlooked. 'I'm sure there's someone else involved.'

'You mean this woman in the lay-by. Could be Nick's lover?' Macy paused to consult the menu.

'Yes, who is she? And why did he have her clothes?' Jo frowned. 'Something is really bothering me about that. You saw the jacket. Was there any blood on it?'

'It looked clean to me but blood would wash off the leather reasonably easily.'

'So why keep it? If Nick knew his girlfriend had worn it to help him do in his old chum, then why keep the jacket?' Jo had to pause to make her order, waiting impatiently while Macy asked questions about the paella. As soon as the waiter left the table, she lowered her voice. 'Do you think Rosie is Nick's lover?'

'She was the bait, do you mean? Nick's accomplice. She gets Sean to that pub in the middle of nowhere, then leaves and phones him to say her car's broken down. Sean drives to help her and gets walloped over the head by Nick. Or by Rosie herself, I suppose. But Rosie has an alibi — of sorts.' Macy sighed and stared out of the window, where the restaurant lights made the dusk seemed deeper. 'These are avenues the police can go down. We have enough to tell our client. That's what concerns me.' Macy came to a halt due to the arrival of his lamb and Jo's paella.

'And what about the suitcase of women's clothes?' Jo went on after a couple of mouthfuls. 'Are they Rosie's? The underwear were all large sizes I noticed. Too big for Rosie. The girl we met at the Royal Shakespeare Theatre was only a twelve at most.'

Macy poured out two glasses of sparkling water. 'What's the paella like? I almost had that but it has to be really freshly made.'

Jo offered him her dish and he took a forkful. 'What about the car?' she said. 'It sounds like the car was bought by the same girl who was in the lay-by. But why would they need a car? Nick had one of his own.'

'Mm, it's good, isn't it?' Macy took another mouthful.

'Or maybe that's too obvious,' Jo went on. 'Nick would not have wanted to use his own car.' She glanced up and saw Macy waiting, fork poised. She pushed her plate more into the centre of the table. 'Look, have some more. It's huge, I can't eat it all.' Eventually she sat back and watched him clear both dishes, which made her smile to herself and wonder how he managed to be in such good shape considering she never saw him do any exercise. In fact, most of the time he actively avoided it. He even toyed with the notion of a pudding but Jo persuaded him they needed to get back on the road. She couldn't change his mind about handing the case over to the police, however.

'I don't want us to get in too deep,' he said when they were waiting for the bill. 'Sean was involved in some sort of fraud, which obviously we don't fully understand. That needs proper investigation. And I don't like the sound of his druggy pals. I don't want to go near any of that.'

When they left the restaurant, Jo noticed that the couple at the next table looked distinctly disappointed.

'I think they were fascinated from the first mention of murder. After that, they looked more at us than each other,' she told Macy on the way to the car.

'I'm not surprised. Violent death is a lot more interesting than true love,' Macy remarked.

On the journey back Jo came up with another loose end for Macy to consider. 'I don't see how it could have been Rosie who bought the Vauxhall. She told us she couldn't drive.'

'You're so good at thinking up these questions — why don't you come up with some answers now and again?' Macy responded. As usual with him, conversation died out when they couldn't find any more to say about the case. They spent most of the journey back to Coventry in silence. Jo was planning how she would get hold of Rosie tomorrow when Macy stopped the car outside her house.

'Do you think I deserve a coffee?' he asked. He was looking across at her, his hands still on the wheel. *Ready to leave in case I say no*, Jo thought. He looked ruffled, tired and attractive.

'OK,' Jo kept her response as minimalist as his but inwardly recognised a little shiver of anticipation. She led the way indoors, opened the door of her flat and was met by Claudius, butting her legs with his large ginger head and wailing. The light on the home phone was flashing and Claudius demanded food.

'If you feed the cat, I'll play your messages back on speaker and get the coffee,' Macy offered.

Jo put down her keys and paused. The cat and the phone could wait a second. She turned to Macy while he was close and put up a hand to the back of his neck, where his hair was very soft. He looked at her seriously before he kissed her. And Jo was glad afterwards she had at least enjoyed one good kiss that night.

She only turned back to Claudius when his pathetic wails could not be ignored any longer. Macy switched on most of the lights while she went to the kitchen, opened a can of cat food and collected the food bowl from the balcony, the cat slowing down the proceedings by winding himself around her legs and generally getting in the way. She heard Macy in the other room pick up the phone.

'Jo, it's Nick.' The tinny voice reached her in the kitchen and she came to the doorway to hear better. 'I hope you don't mind me ringing you at home. I got your number from your application form. I've been thinking about what you said at lunchtime and I'd like to talk to you about it. I'm coming to Coventry tonight. Can you meet me? I'll ring you again when I get there.'

'That was timed at 3.20 p.m.,' Macy said and was interrupted by a second message. This was a woman's voice, bright and cheerful. 'It's Kelly Greenaway. Your jacket is fixed, Jo, and you can pick it up any time. Have you had time to look at my chart yet? What about a consultation at my house soon?' Kelly then left her number and address.

'That's just some astrology work. I've been reinterpreting her chart,' Jo said, pleased that Macy had evidence that her other line of business was still thriving.

Nick's voice, more anxious and almost pleading, cut across her. 'It's Nick again. Please could you come down to the Castaway tonight? You know where it is. I'll be there until late. It's really important that I speak to you. Try and come.'

Jo looked at Macy, who was frowning, his eyes darker than usual. When he looked up, she read his resigned expression and knew her plans for the night were not going to materialise. 'What do you want to do?' he asked as if he had not already decided.

'It's ten to eleven. The Castaway will still be open. If he really is staying late, he should still be there. But as we've just decided that Nick's a possible murderer I'm not daft enough to go on my own. You'll have to come with me.'

'Of course we should go to the police first,' Macy said. 'But whatever we do, we'd better get a move on. However vital he says this is, I don't suppose he'll wait for ever.'

‘We’ll call the police on the way,’ Jo suggested. They left Claudius to his dinner and hurried outside to Macy’s car, where the seats were still warm. Jo glanced at him as he started the engine and wondered if she had guessed right when she’d assumed he would want to try and meet Nick.

There was a keen sense of disappointment in the air, but it was not that which gave her a sliding feeling in the pit of her stomach and found her gripping her seat belt at her chest. As they sped along the A46 towards the woods, queasy memories arose of a flattened and bloodied skull and a man’s white and injured leg hanging off a stretcher. She suddenly felt sure she and Macy had made the wrong decision.

CHAPTER EIGHTEEN

'He must think I've got the notebook,' Jo remarked to Macy when they were within a mile or so of the pub. The lanes were so narrow, the car occasionally bashed the hedgerows on her side.

'Very likely,' was Macy's terse reply. He braked sharply at a stop sign. Once or twice he'd had to pull in to allow other cars to pass, and a cyclist with no lights, which had caused some swearing. Jo peered vainly at all the cars in case she recognised Nick but it was difficult to distinguish the drivers in the dark.

'I thought he was worried when I mentioned it at lunchtime.' Jo felt another twist of unease. 'I sort of implied I had it because I didn't want him to go to Cass for it.'

Macy didn't respond. They approached the pub. A few people were hanging around their cars preparing to leave, and the lights were on inside, but the pub itself was closed. Macy rapped on the door while Jo watched the last few people drive away.

'He's not here.' Her brisk, cheerful tone sounded patently false to her ears. She crossed the car park to look at the only two cars that were left. They probably belonged to the bar staff. 'He must have left,' she called over her shoulder to Macy, who was heading round the back of the pub.

The night was clammy and black, and she resisted the temptation to get back in Macy's car. She noticed something glinting against the driver's door and realised he had left his keys in the ignition. Possibly this was an old PI ruse to enable a fast exit when serving papers but it struck her as unsafe. She removed them, clutching them in her tense fingers as she walked towards the front of the pub. Not sure what she was looking for, she turned over recent events in her mind. Finding Macy's keys had started her worrying about missing details again. She tried the glass doors of the pub but they were firmly locked. Why did the idea of locking things away keep niggling at her?

Possessions are kept under lock and key to keep them safe, she found herself thinking. Or to keep them secret. Away from prying eyes. Although they might seem unimportant to *some* eyes. Like the stash of cash hidden in Cass's make-up bag only got her sacked because the bank police were directed to look there. Or the notebook she stole from Sean's pocket, where the string of numbers which seemed innocuous, meaningless. And the suitcase that had been locked in Nick's boot. Lynne Walmsley had taken the key out of a bedside drawer to open it.

Jo's feet came to a halt in the lane. Suddenly she saw the questions and answers as if they were written across her retina.

How had Lynne been able to unlock the case? She had said she had taken the key off Nick's key ring. But if the suitcase belonged to his lover, why would Nick have the key? And on his key ring? Surely it would be more natural to keep it separate. Wasn't it more likely the suitcase was his? And the clothes . . . which would explain the large sizes.

Jo remembered Carol's face when she saw the underclothes: she had looked as if she had just put two and two together. Maybe this was a secret of Nick's that she had somehow guessed. A PA knows a lot about a person. Hadn't Celia often said something like that to her? And of course if Nick had been dressed as a woman to kill Sean, then maybe he wouldn't have needed an accomplice.

Jo walked slowly away from the pub, letting this sink in. Macy was still nowhere to be seen. She was about to call out for him but became aware of a bass thumping in the distance and the occasional shout, as if there was a party going on somewhere. She looked round at the empty lane and fields beyond and couldn't imagine where. It was the kind of still night when sound carries a long way.

Jo realised she was near the spot where Alan had met her in his car last Friday. She could wait there, as, soon enough, she knew Macy would return. But she glanced around again, checked she had her phone and walked slowly, her low heels sounding loud on the tarmac, towards the track that led to the reservoir. She was rigid with tension and a part of her wanted to give up and return to her flat, saying, 'Ah well, we tried. Now let's go to bed.' She smiled to herself at this idea.

Her eye caught something pale in the bushes below to her right. Down towards the reservoir, she saw the front of a light-coloured car, some distance away and half-hidden. It must be parked just off the track. She moved a few paces forward, her heart hammering and the keys still digging into her fingers.

She came to the gate she remembered from last time. From here she could no longer see the car. The gate was open, despite a notice saying the land belonged to the water authority. Jo hesitated. Was Nick parked down there? If so, God knows what he was doing. Or had he left his car? In which case . . . ?

Behind her, rapid footsteps were hurrying along the lane. Ridiculously, she looked at the nearby scrubby woodland and thought of hiding. She stepped to the side, where she did not feel so vulnerable, her feet finding soft damp grass. After a minute, she was relieved to see it was Macy striding quickly towards her, hands in pockets. She stepped out so as not to startle him but her appearance still brought him up short. He swore feelingly when he saw it was her.

'Ssh! I've seen a car,' she whispered. 'On the track by the lake.' It was too dark to see Macy's face but she felt him sigh.

'Oh, God. Better go and have a look then,' he said, sounding heavy-hearted.

They passed through the gate, with Jo slightly ahead. As soon as they turned off the lane, the night seemed to close in and the beat of the music that Jo had noticed before seemed louder. The track sloped steeply down and, because they couldn't see much, the gravel felt slippy and uncertain. Behind her, Macy slithered once or twice.

The car was parked at the last twist of the lane before the reservoir. The first thing Jo noticed was that the driver's door wasn't closed properly. The lines of the metallic silver body caught what little light there was. Behind the car, the reservoir lay flat and black, almost still. The rock music was distinct now and she suddenly remembered the clubhouse and realised there must be a party going on there. Perhaps Nick had gone to that, she thought.

As she got closer to the car, Jo could see someone sitting in the driving seat. Involuntarily, she came to a halt, knowing she must be in full view. The driver didn't move and the dread that had made her nervous earlier came back, full force. She made her legs start moving forward again.

She approached, sure it was Nick sitting there. From his shoulders, the rounded cheek and the pale hair, he was recognisable as the man she had chatted to at lunchtime. She drew closer.

He was dead.

His hands were resting on the steering wheel. But there was a total stillness about him, which made her teeth start to chatter. She clamped her lips shut and stopped still. Nick Walmsley's head was inclined forward, his mouth open and his eyes strangely protruding.

Macy was following so close he almost walked into her. 'Don't touch anything. We'll get the police. Where's your phone, use the torch.' He walked around the car to the passenger side. Disregarding his own advice, he opened the passenger door using the sleeve of his jacket. The interior light came on.

'Shit.' She fumbled with her phone, suddenly unable to find anything useful on it. Her eyes were drawn to the body. Nick looked as smart as he had when he had left the pub in Richmond. This struck her as odd, almost indecent. The uncanny sense of something jarring, something very wrong kept her transfixed on the scene. Even thoughts failed her, no words in her head except banal ones, which kept repeating themselves. *So peaceful, so apparently peaceful. And yet he is definitely dead.*

Taking a breath, Jo pulled her sleeve over her hand as Macy had done and opened the driver's door, which was already ajar. Once again, the thought recurred, *Peaceful, unharmed.* There was no blood or sign of injury. Maybe it was a heart attack or some other seizure. Her normal, rational brain started to reassert itself, challenging her. Would the body be this neat, sitting upright and apparently calm? She could smell something strange in the car, a faintly medicinal smell, like disinfectant. Back on the rutted track, she could hear Macy calling the police from his phone.

'They're on their way,' he said to her. He followed her gaze. 'The keys are in the ignition, doors and boot unlocked. I can't understand it.'

Jo gently pushed the door closed again, trying to leave it exactly as she had first seen it. From the lake someone shouted.

Jo leaped away from the car, jarring her whole body. The shout was followed by a scream and then a splash.

'Sounds like kids,' Macy commented but Jo noticed he was breathing fast as well. There was another loud splash from behind them followed by raucous shouting and laughter. 'I wonder if they heard anything.' Macy sounded weary. 'The police will find out. We'll wait here and they'll phone when they're close by.'

They fell into silence and Jo kept her eyes on the ground, almost afraid that if she looked at Nick's body, she would become transfixed again. Even in the dark, she noticed that the gravel around the back of the car was churned up, particularly at the back. She thought maybe Nick had manoeuvred the car before parking but the marks were not consistent all the way around. It looked more like there had been a scuffle behind the car. Jo puzzled over this. Nick had looked too neat for a man who had just been in a fight.

'Must be a natural death, do you think?' she wondered aloud. 'A heart attack or a stroke?'

'There would be more mess,' Macy said succinctly. 'Odd timing, too. Just after he called you to meet him here.'

Jo gave an involuntary shudder but her brain went relentlessly on. 'Suicide, then? He took an overdose and drove here to die?'

'More likely. Still should be more mess though. Death is usually pretty messy.'

'And why arrange to meet me and then kill himself?'

'Stop worrying about how he died, the police pathologists will know in hours. Maybe minutes.' He glanced at his watch.

It was not the kind of problem that was so easily dismissed. Jo's mind kept returning to it throughout the long wait to be questioned by the police. They soon turfed the landlord of the Castaway out of his bed and set up a mini headquarters in the pub lounge. Matti, while distinctly grouchy to start with, gradually became resigned to his temporary role and switched on the lights and heating and made endless coffee. He even offered brandy, which was turned down by all except Macy.

The coffee was very strong and a lot more to Jo's taste than the brandy. A pale, tired-looking officer in an overcoat had told Jo and Macy where to wait and, as other squad cars and SOCO vans arrived in the car park, he directed uniformed police and the forensic teams back along the lane in what seemed like droves. Eventually an unknown detective sergeant came over to question them and take statements, and they were finally allowed to leave the pub at three thirty a.m. with instructions to report to Inspector Cash at Coventry police station the next day.

Jo and Macy went back to her flat. It seemed too late for Macy to go home so they both lay on her bed, only half-undressed, and slept a stupefied sleep until past nine, when Jo awoke to the sound of her phone ringing.

CHAPTER NINETEEN

Jo was greeted by a cheery voice reminding her that she was due at the police station, 'At 11.15 am, please.' As it was mainly due to the police that they had got in so late, Jo's assurance that she would be there as soon as possible was given through gritted teeth. She put the phone down and went off to make coffee.

In the shower, it occurred to her that the police would be interested in the messages Nick had left on her voicemail. As soon as she was dressed she replayed them to see if they brought any enlightenment. Nick's voice sounded anxious, almost pleading, but Jo could not deduce anything else. She downloaded the messages onto her mobile, realising the police would want to know what Nick had said. And it would certainly not do any harm to have proof of why she and Macy were snooping around near the dead body last night.

She sat down with another coffee, opened her laptop and tried to put the night's events out of her mind. The case was now with the police. There was her own business to run — she still had to write her newsletter and this week's astrology column. Her friend Hanni had emailed her to invite her to a Mind, Body and Spirit evening in the Cotswolds. *I've got you a great position near the entrance and you're the only astrologer there, so you can offer all your wonderful services*, Hanni had enthused in her email.

It reminded Jo that she must arrange to see Kelly Greenaway. She found her report on Kelly's chart and put it into a presentation folder, then rang Kelly and offered to deliver them late that afternoon, allowing plenty of time at the police station. Kelly suggested six o'clock because her husband Mark was on 'bath and bed duty' for their young daughter that evening. This settled, Jo made a start on her weekly prediction column. She looked up the position of the planets for the coming week and saw that Mercury and Saturn had moved out of opposition, so at least it should be an easier week than the last one. She had got as far as Leo when Macy appeared from the bedroom.

'There's coffee in the kitchen and plenty of hot water,' Jo said and Macy went robotically in the direction of the bathroom. Jo was working on Scorpio by the time he re-emerged looking more human. 'You don't want any breakfast, do you?' Jo asked. 'The police have been on the phone and they want us to go down there at eleven.'

'I never eat breakfast,' Macy said as one stating an article of faith. 'But have you got any tea? I can't take any more coffee — I feel like I've been drinking it all night.'

Jo left her work to hunt for the teapot, something she only used when her mother visited. 'Do you think they'll keep us long at the police station?' she asked from under the sink.

'Well, yes — if last night is anything to go by. I think they're a bit stumped by Nick's death.' Macy stretched and sat at her kitchen table.

'Last night I heard the inspector say it must be a heart attack.' She filled the kettle and started searching for the tea bags. 'But why was he driving his car down that lane? Unless maybe he was feeling bad and pulled off the road . . .'

'They'll be asking for a post-mortem anyway but I doubt if they'll know the outcome yet. This morning they will just want us to run through what we know about Nick and Sean, which will mean explaining all that stuff about the fraud at the bank.'

'Will you mention the women's clothes?' Jo had a look in the fridge in case there was anything in there which she could offer Macy. There was a lump of cheese and an out-of-date yoghurt. She closed the door again.

'Yes, there's no point in keeping things back. See what *they* make of it.' Macy added with some relish, 'We'll explain about the notebook too because that makes it clear not only what Nick was doing at the Castaway but what *we* were doing there.'

Jo bit her lip. 'That means involving Cass.'

'She's already involved.'

Jo saw that Macy's instinct for self-preservation was as strong as ever. She poured him a cup of tea and went to collect her laptop. No doubt there would be hours of waiting at the police station and she would get a chance to carry on working on the interpretation of Kelly's chart there.

'How is it going? The zodiac stuff? Are you doing more consultations now?' Macy asked, watching her through the kitchen doorway.

Jo explained about Kelly Greenaway. Interpretation of a natal chart was the area of astrology Jo enjoyed the most and she was looking forward to the consultation. 'This is the area of work I really want to get into. And Kelly's a really interesting character,' she went on. 'I've remembered why she seemed familiar when I met her.'

'Yes, you mentioned it and I went back to the office and looked it up. Her kid was kidnapped, wasn't she?'

The kidnapping had been a big local news story about a year ago and it had come back to Jo when she'd been working on Kelly's chart. 'The little girl was only about two. But they got her back, didn't they? And she was unscathed.'

Macy nodded. He took a professional interest in local crime. 'They found the kid in a caravan near Bedworth with some weirdo. Of course, the Greenaways are minted. Well, Mark Greenaway is. They stumped up the ransom.'

'That's right. It's fascinating because all this is in Kelly's chart.' Jo continued. 'There are definite indications of dramatic family upheavals. It's unusual to have the Sun and Moon both in the Eighth House. And the influence of Pluto is very strong.' She glanced up and saw Macy's eyes had a glazed look. She also noticed that he had finished his tea. She changed the subject and told him her theory that Nick used the women's clothes himself. 'He could have been the person in the lay-by.'

Macy frowned. 'I suppose from the back, bending over the bonnet of a car, he might be mistaken for a woman,' he mused. 'But that still doesn't explain why he would keep the clothes.'

'Because maybe they weren't just the clothes he did the murder in. Maybe they were his outfits. And if he was into wearing women's clothes, I am betting Carol, his PA, would know more about it.'

'Possibly. Come on, let's go and dump these problems on the police.' Macy stood up, straightened his rumpled clothes and pronounced himself ready to go. He and Jo were on their way out of the flat when her phone rang. She answered it frostily, thinking it was another reminder from the police.

'Jo — is Macy with you?' Alan's voice sounded more than usually brusque. When Jo hesitated for a split second, he carried straight on, 'It's the only other place I can think of. I've tried his usual haunts.' Jo felt her eyebrows rising involuntarily at this but she did not interrupt. 'He'll throw a wobbly when he finds out: Connor Fitzpatrick's gone missing. His elder brother's just been on the phone. Connor's been gone since yesterday. Nobody knows where he is and his house has been turned over. What's more, he still owes us money.'

'Macy's here, you'd better speak to him.' Jo handed over the phone. Her first thought was that Sean's debtors had decided to carry out their threats.

Contrary to Alan's expectations, Macy's reaction was calm and mild. He listened to Alan in silence most of the time, jotted down a phone number and promised to meet him at the office later. But he was frowning when he ended the call. 'I hate it when something happens to one of our clients,' he grumbled, adding more briskly, 'Kieran Fitzpatrick called the office this morning. I suppose I'd better speak to him.' He started to dial the number and Jo glanced at her watch.

'I'll drive us then. You'd better be quick, they won't like it at the station if we keep them waiting,' Jo said. 'And could you ask him a favour for me?' Despite worrying about Connor, a handy solution to another little problem had occurred to her. 'Will you ask him to send us a photograph of Sean's wedding?'

Macy shot her a doubtful look but, characteristically, didn't give her the pleasure of explaining her theory. He was polite and efficient with Kieran. She guessed that the break-in at Connor's house was caused by the dealer who was owed money. Maybe his patience had run out and he was looking for things he could take instead. This idea seemed to be confirmed when Macy finished the conversation. He told her that a laptop and cash had been taken from Connor's house.

'Did Kieran promise to send the wedding photo?' Jo asked.

'No problem. He'll email one later. He thinks I'm mad of course but—' Macy lifted his hands. 'We'd better go or they'll be sending a squad car for us.'

'I think Rosie could be the woman Sean married,' Jo explained on the way downstairs, unable to keep quiet about this theory any longer. 'She's got to fit in somewhere. Otherwise, why did she meet him in the pub? And I'm sure she helped Nick kill him by phoning about the car breakdown. Although maybe she didn't know that was what Nick was going to do. Either way, we should try and find her.'

'Maybe later if you like,' Macy said, 'depending on what the police say and what time we're finished at the station.'

In fact it was past four when Jo was told she could go. The detective from the drugs squad who had been making her go over every detail of her late-night conversation with Connor told her Macy had left an hour ago. Jo only had a couple of hours before her appointment with Kelly in Leamington but she was still determined to make an effort to find Rosie. The first thing to try was Rosie's phone number, which she had noted down and left in her car. She walked across to where she had parked it and was surprised to see Macy leaning against the passenger door.

'I only popped back to the office for a change of clothes. Anita said they would be finished with you in an hour or so. I thought you wanted to tie up this loose end and find Rosie? She's at the Midlands Dance Championships in Birmingham. If you want to drive us there, I'll tell you how I know.'

Jo felt slightly disgruntled to have the initiative taken away from her but she fell in with Macy's plans with a good grace. As she drove onto the ring road, she pointed out that she would have to be in Leamington for six.

'Shouldn't be any problem.' Macy seemed in good spirits.

She looked over at him. 'You'd better tell me where we're going, then.'

CHAPTER TWENTY

The Baptist Central Hall was not easy to find and Jo had already made two U-turns before they finally arrived at the building, which was a converted cinema surrounded by a mix of restaurants and takeaways from Indian to Thai to fried chicken. She parked outside the Thai place and followed Macy through double doors at the back of the foyer. They were met by a small man in a black tie and dinner jacket, who was standing by a desk in the corridor.

'Are these the Midlands Dance Championships?' Macy asked.

'Yes, sir.' The man smiled through a neat beard. 'Name, sir, please?' He consulted an open book on the desk in front of him. 'Are you a member?'

'We're from the *Birmingham Evening News*,' Macy said. 'Down here, is it?' He started along the corridor and the smart bearded man did not object.

Jo peered through the round windows in the old cinema doors at the end of the corridor. There was a stage and a small band at the far end of the large room. A cluster of overdressed men and women were dancing in the space where the seats used to be. Other people stood around looking either bored or tense.

She pushed open the doors and was met by a blast of music from the speakers. They walked past the dancers, who were flouncing up and down in time to the surprisingly raucous Latin American beat, the men thrusting out hairless chests.

'Half these are just kids,' Macy observed as he side-stepped to avoid a cerise skirt sticking out two feet either side of the diminutive girl wearing it.

'Do you want a drink?' Jo asked. 'There's a bar over there.'

Macy agreed and they took their drinks to an unsteady table at the edge of the dance floor just as the music finished. The six or seven couples struck various attitudes and then tripped off the floor, clinging to each other's hands and smiling aggressively. While the smooth voice of an MC filled in the gap between dances, Jo looked around for Rosie and Dean.

'Excuse me, can I sit here a minute?' A woman flashed a smile at them over a low-cut black dress. 'It's just that I'm having a wardrobe malfunction with my dance shoes.' She bent over and fiddled with one patent leather shoe. She seemed older than a lot of the competitors and a thick leg showed through the slit in her dress. Macy asked if she knew where he could find Rosie Martell.

'Still in the dressing room, I should think.' The woman was trying to loosen her gold buckle. 'She'll be out for the tango in a minute if you hang on.' The MC called the next dancers to the floor and she beamed at Macy. 'Thank you, love.' She turned and hissed at her partner, who was hovering behind her, and they stepped onto the dance floor.

Jo noticed Dean first, with his distinctive, long parted hair, threading his way through a crowd of people near the bar.

'Here's Dean,' Macy murmured. 'Now where's Torvill?'

Rosie came into view from behind a pillar, holding on to Dean's frilly shirt sleeve. Macy must have caught her eye because she looked in their direction and away again quickly.

Dean had stopped to speak to someone and she waited near him. After half a minute, she risked another look. She said something to Dean and started towards their table.

'What are you doing here?' she asked. Her wide eyes were challenging but her hands looked nervous. 'Taking an interest in the dancing, are you?'

'You remember us, then?' Macy stood up and pulled up a spare chair for her. 'Can we have a chat?'

'Not now,' Rosie said. 'We're due to go on next. Couldn't you have chosen a better time?'

'Nick Walmsley's dead,' Jo said by way of explanation.

Rosie was looking around at the other dancers. 'Who's he?'

'Sean's boss from the bank. You know that, don't you?' Jo went on.

'Never heard of him. And I don't know what you're after, but—'

'Just a talk.' Macy held her gaze. 'You said you didn't know Sean Fitzpatrick but he had your number in a notebook.'

Rosie's hands, which had been playing with a silk flower on her dress, suddenly became still and some of the nerve went out of her face. 'You what?' she said.

The dance was finishing and Dean came up looking worried. 'Come on, Rosie. This is no time to get stuck in conversation.' He glared at Jo and Macy but apparently didn't remember them. Or didn't choose to. 'We're on now.'

'I'll stay here.' Macy sat and took his bottle of beer. 'Will you speak to me afterwards?'

Rosie gave them an uncertain look and Dean grabbed her hand. 'What the hell is going on?' He jabbed a finger at Macy. 'If you've ballsed this up for us . . .' His sentence trailed off and he tugged Rosie towards the dance floor.

'You know Rosie's name isn't in Sean's little book,' Jo said.

'That's true,' Macy agreed, 'but Rosie doesn't know what's in it.'

'She looks worried,' Jo said, watching her dance. 'Let's hope we can prise her away from Dean and get her to tell us what she knows.' She looked at her watch, calculating on the time she needed to allow to get to Leamington. She was not about to let this PI work interfere with her proper business of being an astrologer, she reminded herself.

When they left the dance floor, Rosie turned towards them, still wearing a fixed smile, and mouthed, 'Five minutes.'

Jo tried to be patient while waiting for Rosie to appear. She came out eventually, having changed into a lurid strapless dress with a stiff skirt, and made her way to their table.

'How did you do?' Jo asked.

'Not bad at all, in the circumstances,' Rosie said. Her face was still shiny with sweat after dancing but her stare was icy. 'Dean's furious with you.' She held her long hair back from her face to cool down. Looking from Jo to Macy, she said, with the return of her usual cheek, 'Are you going to buy me a drink now?'

'All right.' Macy got to his feet.

'Bacardi and Coke, please,' Rosie said. 'I can have one now we've finished the big number.' Macy went to the bar. 'What do you want, then?' she added to Jo.

'Just for you to tell us what you were doing with Sean at the Castaway on the eighteenth of June.'

'Or?' Rosie eyed her, head on one side. 'What will you do if I don't tell you?'

'We'll take Sean's little book to the police.'

Macy brought the drink over. She took a mouthful and stared at them. 'I don't believe you for a minute. But I knew it'd have to come out. So I may as well tell you as anyone.' She got up, carrying her drink. 'Come on. We'll go outside where it's cooler.' Jo and Macy exchanged a glance and followed her.

'I did know Sean,' Rosie said matter-of-factly as she made her way towards a fire exit. 'He used to come to Leamington on business about once a month — so he said. I met him at the club where I work part-time. He took me out a few times — mainly to casinos and night clubs. I quite enjoyed my little self, really.' She leaned back on the metal bar to open the door.

'But . . .?' Jo prompted. They followed her out into the car park, which was deserted.

'But he was just messing me about,' Rosie sighed. 'He would use my flat as somewhere to stay. It wasn't me he was interested in.' She found a wall to sit on. She sipped her drink and looked up at Macy, doe-eyed. 'Ciggie?'

He produced a packet. Rosie took a cigarette and a light. 'You're a good listener,' she commented.

Macy shrugged. 'Part of the job.' He sat down next to her and lit a cigarette for himself. 'Tell me what you were doing in the Castaway.'

'Oh yes. Well, you've got the picture about Sean and me, haven't you? He was getting fed up with me. What he didn't know is, I got pregnant.' Rosie looked at Jo and shook her head, her long blonde hair falling in front of her face. She pushed it back again. 'My own stupid fault, but obviously I still held him partly responsible. By the time I knew for sure, Sean was hardly speaking to me. I still saw him at the club but he wasn't staying in my flat anymore or taking me out. I knew he was loaded and I wanted him to pay for the termination. I wanted it done privately — the best place I could.' She paused, looking down at the grimy pavement. 'This makes me sound awful, doesn't it?'

'No — just practical,' Jo said.

Rosie gave a laugh. 'Well, that wasn't what Sean said when I told him. First of all, I had to find a way of getting him to talk to me in private—'

'Rosie! For God's sake — it's the formation number next,' Dean's anguished voice cut across the car park. He was leaning out of the door.

'Got to go,' Rosie said. She stubbed out her cigarette in the empty glass and waved to Dean.

'If we wait here, will you come back and tell us the rest?' Macy asked.

'Well, I've started so I may as well bloody finish.' Rosie gave them one more look and hurried back indoors.

Jo sighed and looked at her watch. 'I can't wait,' she said, 'I mustn't miss my appointment with Kelly.' She felt guilty but she had promised herself that her astrology business would not be sacrificed to PI work.

Macy shrugged. 'I'll wait here, then. It looks like she met Sean in the pub, doesn't it? But I doubt if she had any more to do with it than that.'

'How will you get back?' she asked to appease her conscience.

'Train, I suppose. Or cab. Don't worry, I won't be helpless without you.'

Jo didn't argue. As she walked to her car, she wondered uncharitably if Macy was staying behind because he fancied Rosie. This didn't occupy her for long, though, as there were more important things to worry her. She knew she would have to drive speedily to get to Kelly's on time.

* * *

It wasn't long before Rosie came out, carrying another drink and trailing a turquoise ostrich feather. Macy was still sitting on the wall.

'Where was I?' She took her place beside him.

'You were trying to get a word with Sean in private.'

'I said you were a good listener.' She glanced up at him and held out her hand. He handed her a cigarette and lit it for her. After a couple of inhalations, she said, 'You know, Deano and I weren't at all bad today. Anyway, as I was saying—' she took another drag — 'I probably would never have seen the bastard again but he couldn't keep away from the club. He was mad about my boss. Although *she* couldn't be bothered with him.'

'Hang on — I'm lost. What's this club?'

'Sorry, I'm rabbiting on, aren't I? This is the sports club where I work that I'm on about now. Kelly's my boss. She owns the place.'

'Who?' Macy interrupted again.

'Kelly Greenaway. I work at her club as a receptionist in the mornings. She lets me use her dance studio to practise in but she gets her pound of flesh in return. Right little tyrant she is, but Sean couldn't get enough of her. He was always pestering her to meet him. Anyway, I heard them arrange to go for a drink that night in the pub. I guessed he would be there first because he seemed so — you know — eager.' Rosie paused to finish her drink. 'All I did was turn up at the Castaway early and I had a right go at Sean, told him what had happened. He got quite nasty, told me to get lost and wouldn't give me any money.' She came to a halt.

'Go on,' Macy said.

'Well, this is the bad bit.' She looked at the uneven gravel of the car park. 'While I was there, he had a phone call. He had to go to the bar to take it. I just put my hand in his jacket pocket. He had a hundred quid in his wallet. I took it. The shit deserved it,' Rosie concluded.

'And then you had to leave before he realised?'

Rosie nodded. 'While he was still on the phone,' she said. 'It was a bit of a shock, I must admit, when you told me he was dead. I thought my jaw must have hit the table but you didn't seem to notice so I said nothing.'

'And you didn't tell the police?'

'They didn't ask me until this morning, funnily enough, when they came to the club. I didn't want them to know the whole story — it doesn't put me in a very good light, does it? And it's none of their business.' Rosie paused and added defensively, 'Anyway Kelly told me to act like Sean had never been near the place because she wanted to protect the good name of the club.' She sighed. 'Well, that's just about it really.'

'You told us you didn't work at Greenaways,' Macy said.

'Yes, I did, didn't I? I was shit-scared, to be honest. You come up and tell me Sean's dead — it's a wonder I didn't have a heart attack. My first thought was to have as little to do with it as possible so I denied all knowledge.'

Macy touched her arm. 'Thanks for telling me all this. I'll try not to tell anyone else. I might go and see your boss, though — will she be at the club?'

Rosie took Macy's wrist and looked at his watch. 'No. It closes early tonight. She'll probably be at home, which is just round the corner from the club.' She told Macy the address as they walked back across the car park. 'What do you want to see Kelly for?'

Macy was saved an explanation by Dean's reappearance in the doorway, telling Rosie to hurry up and get changed because the minibus was waiting. She swore. 'He's a right little bully, isn't he? I've got a nose for them.'

CHAPTER TWENTY-ONE

Weaving through the rush-hour traffic on the ring road, Jo was annoyed with herself for leaving so little time to get to Kelly's. Especially when this was exactly the kind of business she wanted as an astrologer.

She could have done without the added stress of being late. Kelly had proved to be a difficult enough subject to study. Jo had been right in thinking that her chart would be interesting. She was a typical cool-headed Aquarian in some ways, unconventional and quick-thinking and with a good business sense, as Jo had expected. But most Aquarians Jo had met were interested in people — they usually embraced many weird friends and causes — whereas Kelly's chart showed her to be self-absorbed. Her Ascendant and a cluster of planets in Aries made her egocentric and tough — reckless, even. There was no doubt about her ambition, either. With Capricorn at the Midheaven, Kelly was aspirational and a social climber and this went along with indications of a deprived or difficult childhood. Jo had been working on a tactful way of putting over some of these unflattering characteristics, knowing Kelly was too shrewd to be easily deceived. She also had the onerous task of pointing out that the immediate future looked fraught. It wasn't going to be a particularly easy consultation.

To increase her blood pressure further, all the traffic lights on the way to Earlsdon were against her and what she thought was a shortcut beside Spencer Park turned out to be blocked by roadworks. While waiting at another red light, she decided that the first thing she needed to do when she had a better idea of how long the journey would take her was to ring Kelly to apologise for being late.

She parked the car at the kerb and raced indoors, grabbing the post from her letter box and taking the stairs two at a time. It only took her a minute to locate the folder with Kelly's birth chart, which she had prepared.

Once on the way to Leamington, Jo called her new client from the car, full of apologies. Kelly was very relaxed about it, saying that she had only just got her daughter to bed anyway so it didn't matter if she was a bit late. Jo promised she should be there in a quarter of an hour and turned her attention to driving.

Stuck at a red light on the Kenilworth Road, her eyes fell on the mail she had picked up at her flat. She hadn't meant to bring it but it must have got caught up in the folders she was carrying. One of the letters caught her attention. She picked it up as the lights changed and instantly dropped it again. The envelope was handwritten in ink and it had the heavy feel of expensive paper. The post mark was London SW15.

Jo parked in front of Greenaways. No matter how many more minutes late it made her, Jo took a moment to take a breath. Then she picked the envelope up, ran her thumb along the top and took out a single piece of notepaper and a cheque.

Dear Jo,

What do they say about heat and kitchens? Anyway, I'm going to Dublin for a while. This serves the purpose of getting me out of the way while I try to borrow the money to pay off Sean's debtors. I'm hoping that you and Macy find a way of getting the buggers locked up but I will pay them if it comes to it.

I enclose a cheque so you can carry on the work and I can be reached at the Dublin address above if you have any news. Better still, write to say you're coming to see me. I'll let my family know where I am.

Don't think too unkindly of me,

Connor

She felt her throat tighten after she had read the last line. She looked at the cheque to distract herself. It was made payable to Macy and Wilson and was reasonably generous. She knew she would not be going to Dublin but she couldn't help a sneaking liking for Connor.

Before she set out to see Kelly, she rang Macy. He didn't pick up so she left a succinct message saying she had heard from Connor. She supposed Macy would write to him, explaining Nick's involvement and death — and the information about the burglary. Connor could presumably come back if the police found Sean's drug suppliers or if they thought he would be safe.

Kelly did not live far from the club and Jo walked the short distance along a wide, quiet road. The houses were set back behind a line of trees so it was difficult to see the numbers. She stepped out onto the grass verge and walked along, peering up drives until she came to number 118.

It was a substantial detached house, built in the 1930s, Jo guessed, in a solid, appealing style with lots of small windows and a roof that swept down to cover the porch. It was the kind of house Jo imagined living in when she indulged in a mental fantasy about being happily married with a brood of kids. Thank God it was just a fantasy, she thought, as she pressed the doorbell.

Kelly's husband opened the door. He was a tall, burly man with a florid complexion and a not-unhandsome face. He looked older than Kelly — in his forties, Jo guessed. He made rather strained small talk as he showed her into a large room at the front of the house, where Kelly was watching television. Sitting on the huge sofa, with her legs tucked underneath her, she looked even more diminutive than Jo remembered.

'Hello at last. I've been looking forward to this evening.' Kelly smiled up at her. 'Fancy making me wait — I would have thought you astrologers could foresee problems so you never got delayed.'

Jo apologised again but Kelly didn't seem to listen. 'You two haven't met, have you?' she said before Jo had finished speaking. 'This is my husband, Mark.' She stood up, putting her arm round his waist, which drew attention to the contrast between her neat, blonde figure and his dark, large one.

'I've got some coffee ready, could you make it for us?' She looked up at Mark. 'I thought Jo and I would go into the morning room. You'll be able to watch the television then, won't you?' Kelly's voice descended into baby talk when she addressed her husband, Jo noticed disapprovingly. But he just smiled at her fondly and went off to make the coffee while Kelly led the way into a little room on the opposite side of the hall. Jo, who was only slightly taller than average, felt large and ungainly following behind Kelly's compact figure, which was clad in an expensive-looking jogging suit.

Jo settled down beside Kelly at the polished wooden desk and took out her notes. She launched into her interpretation, highlighting Kelly's positive points — her organisational skills, her courage and resourcefulness. Jo's own enthusiasm for the subject came through and Kelly was a good listener. Jo drank two cups of coffee from a cafetière supplied by Mark and she was so engrossed that she hardly noticed how good it was.

They were coming to the end when they were interrupted by a child's crying from upstairs. Kelly looked up but before she could move, Mark popped his head round the door to say he would go to see what was wrong. Kelly turned to Jo, relieved. 'Poor Nuala. She still gets nightmares after her ordeal.'

'I remember hearing about it on the news.' Jo put her notes together and passed the presentation folder to Kelly. 'You must have been worried to death.'

'I was.' Kelly nodded, a shadow passing over her regular features. 'I even made an appeal on television, I was so desperate. I never really thought we would get her back.' She paused, her face tight with the memory, then she looked back at Jo and seemed to gather herself again. 'Thank you for this work. I'm very pleased — you've said all sorts of things about me which I recognise. Now, I've had your jacket mended and it's as good as new. It's at the club. Do you fancy a walk over there to get it?'

'My car's there anyway,' Jo said. The little room was becoming stuffy and the idea of a walk appealed. Kelly went upstairs to tell Mark where they were going and came down carrying a rolled towel under her arm. 'He's reading her stories,' Kelly smiled as she opened the front door. 'I told him I was going for a swim. I often go over in the evenings when the club's closed. It's the only time I get to use the facilities myself. Have you thought any more about joining?'

'Oh, I don't think I can afford it,' Jo said. She had almost forgotten that she had said she wanted to be a member when she had been snooping around the place. Kelly accepted her answer with a little nod and they walked on in silence for a while.

'It's funny, but do you remember the chap who gave you the recommendation to this place?' Kelly said as they walked up the steps to the club. 'Sean Fitzpatrick, wasn't it? The police were here today asking about him — if I knew him, if he was a member and so on. Have they been to see you?'

'Not exactly. I've been to see them.' Jo decided she might as well admit her involvement. While Kelly let them in and led her into the kitchen, she explained that she had been working for Sean Fitzpatrick's brother. Kelly seemed to be only half-listening. She found the jacket and handed it over while Jo was talking.

'Tell you what,' she said when Jo had paused for breath, 'why don't you come for a swim, I remember you said you liked swimming. I've got a spare costume. You won't get a chance to use an empty pool like ours very often.'

Jo looked up from examining her jacket, which seemed as good as new. Although it was early in the evening, she felt strangely tired. But Kelly was insistent and Jo eventually agreed. It seemed an odd idea but it had been a hot day and a few lengths in the luxury pool might be quite pleasant.

Kelly looked pleased. 'I'll go and get a costume. See you down at the pool.'

Kelly went off cheerfully and Jo, smothering a yawn, made her way to the basement. She remembered the way down the dim flight of stairs. There was just enough light from the windows above not to need a light on. She hesitated at the bottom, wondering which set of double doors led to the pool. In that second, she heard a noise, like a murmur or a stifled laugh but strangely echoing. It seemed to come from ahead of her.

She pushed the door nearest to the direction of the noise and heard it again. It sounded like someone groaning this time. The pool lay dark and undisturbed in front of her, the tiled, cavernous space around it undisturbed and empty. The whirlpool bath was still. She wondered where to find a light switch.

She heard a gasp and a scuffle. There was someone else there in the room. Her mouth went dry.

She didn't call out. But she knew whoever was there must have heard her come in. She was moving along beside the wall, feeling desperately for a light switch. All she could feel beneath her fingers were smooth tiles. Not far in front of her, she thought she saw some movement but she couldn't work out what.

Her hand found a switch. In an instant, the place was lit up, white light bouncing off blue water. Jo was staring straight ahead at a couple on the floor, lying in an embrace and frozen with anxiety. A woman disentangled herself and sat up, meeting Jo's eyes with a rueful expression and struggling back into her swimming costume, which she was only half-wearing. 'Who on earth are you?' she asked, her voice wary. Her partner raised herself on one elbow and looked up at Jo through untidy long hair.

The sudden relief that she was not under any threat made Jo feel light-headed for a second but in that time she remembered who the first woman was. It was Jane, who had been at the reception desk when Jo had first tried to get in the club.

'I'm here with Kelly,' Jo said. 'What are you doing here? I thought this place was closed.'

'Don't tell Kelly, will you, for God's sake?' Jane said. 'She'd definitely sack me.'

'She'll be here any minute,' Jo warned.

Both women were now on their feet and scrambling into towelling robes. 'There's a way out this way.' Jane grabbed her partner's hand and headed to the back of the pool. The other woman, whom Jo did not recognise, remained quiet throughout, following Jane without question. 'Please don't say anything, will you?' Jane pleaded as they hurried past, barefoot. 'We don't do this very often but Kelly doesn't normally come down here at night.'

'Of course,' Jo said. The two women hurried out past the locker room and Jo found a bench to sit on. Whether it was the shock of disturbing the women or simply her late night last night, she felt tired and detached. She wondered if she was coming down with flu and something else bothered her. Jane had said Kelly didn't usually go down to the pool but Kelly had said she often went swimming at night.

She was still pummelling her slow brain into puzzling this out when Kelly arrived carrying a towel and swimsuit. 'You're about a size ten, aren't you?' She didn't say what had delayed her and Jo realised that was probably because nothing had. Jane and her partner had only taken seconds to leave.

Jo felt less like the idea of swimming now but she didn't have the energy to argue with Kelly. She went to the locker rooms and put on her costume, leaving her clothes neatly folded on a bench. Kelly was already in the water when Jo came out. The lights seemed so bright after the locker room that her eyes hurt. She was consumed with a desire to lie down and go to sleep and suddenly decided it would not be a good idea to swim when she felt like this. She had better go home and go to bed, she thought.

'I'm going to give it a miss,' she called to Kelly, 'I'm not feeling too good. I'll let myself out, don't worry.' She turned back to the locker room but Kelly hauled herself out of the pool and came up to her. Kelly's face, dripping with water, looked up at her. 'What's wrong? Can I get you anything?'

'No, nothing,' Jo smiled, 'I just feel I might be coming down with something, that's all—'

Kelly put a hand on her arm. 'Are you sure? Let's see if you've got a temperature.' She put her other hand up to Jo's forehead in an almost maternal gesture. Jo submitted to this concern reluctantly, longing to be home and horizontal. Then the grip on her arm tightened. She stepped back and Kelly's other hand grabbed a fistful of her hair.

Jo's scalp felt like it was parting from her head. She let out an involuntary yell. Before she could struggle free, Kelly shoved her towards the pool. She grabbed at thin air, made contact with Kelly's shoulder and fell, bringing Kelly on top of her. They hit the water with a painful crash. Then Jo went under.

Kelly's hands grabbed at her and caught hold of her legs. Jo broke the surface, thrashing her arms, gasping for breath. Her shocked and bemused brain remembered that Jane and partner couldn't be all that far away so she forced a scream out of her throat. It echoed round the deserted pool. Kelly ducked her. This time she swallowed water. She could feel the strong fingers pressing on the top of her head. She writhed, fighting with her whole body to get away.

Random thoughts came to her while the pressure of water pounded her head. *This is how Kelly killed Nick. That was the funny smell in his car: chlorine. She's going to kill me too.*

One of her kicks caught Kelly in the stomach and the hands came off her head for a moment. Jo struggled upwards.

The world above the water seemed to be tilting from side to side dangerously but Jo made out the side of the pool and headed for it. Jo was a reasonable swimmer but Kelly was a better one and began to catch her up.

There was no bar along the side of the pool, in fact, not much to hold on to at all, just a lip in the floor tiles. Jo reached for that. One hand made contact with the grainy wet tiles, one shoulder was out. She yelled again at the top of her voice. Kelly's hands gripped around her legs.

'It's no good,' Jo gasped. 'I'm sending for your wedding pictures. Everyone'll see them—' Jo made another lunge for the side, hoping to pull herself out.

But Kelly had not given up. She launched herself at Jo. Her doll-like face and staring eyes hovered above Jo for a second and then she drove her full weight down.

Jo could see nothing but water and felt the pressure of Kelly's thumbs on her throat, squeezing so hard, the breath wouldn't come.

CHAPTER TWENTY-TWO

Piercing lights swayed above her eyes. She could hear nothing at all. Then blackness. Then the lights again, shifting high up, and cold water lapping her face. From somewhere, her mind produced the thought that she was floating. That meant she could turn over and start swimming. Still deaf and dazed, Jo tried this and the side of the pool came into view — but miles away. One stroke and then another. Arms heavy, white tiles in front, wavering and reappearing like wavy lines in her head.

She touched them. Cold, certain. She raised an arm to try to haul herself out but someone grabbed it. She tried to pull away, failed and blacked out again. When she opened her eyes, Jane's concerned face was hovering over her. The pain in her chest pinned her to the tiled floor and the pounding was back in her head. Jo retched and water spurted out of her mouth. Jane's face went away. Someone was making a disgusting gurgling noise and someone else was speaking. She heard Macy's voice, soft and low-pitched. But she must be imagining that, her brain told her. A woman said she had phoned an ambulance.

'I'm not going to hospital,' Jo muttered, 'I've got a phobia about hospitals.' She meant this to be an amusing remark but it came out as an incoherent noise. Jane's face reappeared and Jo recognised her Australian accent but couldn't distinguish the words.

She was aware of the stretcher and throwing up more water and the ambulance. The motion was horrible. This time the ceiling really was moving about, Jo reassured herself, and she could hear Macy again but couldn't see him.

When she woke up properly he was definitely there. The walls around her were so bare that it could only be a hospital. There were screens in one corner and blinds at the window. Macy was standing with his back to her. He seemed to be peering through the blinds. She lay for a while and watched him and noticed that the pain in her chest seemed to have moved up to her throat. It hurt to move anything.

Jo was so glad to see him that it made her irritable. 'What are you doing here?' she tried to say and was pleased to notice that the words came out correctly, even though her voice was unrecognisable.

Macy turned round. 'I'm staying out of the way of the police. Alan's speaking to them, relating our successes. It's his big moment,' he said. 'How are you feeling?' He came over and looked down at her.

'Terrible. Where am I?' Jo croaked.

'In a recovery room at the Walsgrave. I asked for you to be allowed to stay on your own, seeing as you've got a phobia about hospitals.'

This forced a grin out of Jo but it was disturbing to discover that anything but very shallow breathing hurt her chest. Her throat didn't want her to speak but she had some information to impart, so she made an effort.

'Kelly was Sean's wife,' she said. 'It came to me when she threw me in the pool.'

'A brilliant piece of deduction,' Macy said, 'although your timing was rubbish.'

'What happened?' Her mind was trying to put together a logical sequence of events after she was thrown in the pool.

'Unfortunately Rosie waited until after you left before letting out the crucial information — that it was Kelly Sean was coming here to see. So I called the police, knowing you were going to meet her. Then I extravagantly caught a taxi and beat them to it, because they went to her house and we went to the club. Oh, I asked Alan to meet me there too. Safety in numbers,' he added with a serious smile.

'And there was I, being half-drowned.' Jo swallowed painfully. 'I'm sure she gave me a sedative or something in that coffee she made. I noticed she didn't drink any—'

'Do you want a drink? There's some water here.' He poured her out a glass, while Jo shifted gently into a more upright position. She took the glass with stiff fingers and drank. 'Alan and I rushed to your rescue,' Macy went on, 'but that fierce Australian girl was seeing to you so we went upstairs and found Kelly stuffing money into a sports bag. Planning another flit, I think.'

'You spoke to her?'

'Only briefly until the police turned up.' Macy sat on the edge of the bed. 'Inspector Merson told me she hadn't even got a divorce from Sean.'

'She's a bigamist?' Jo's sore throat forced her to be succinct.

'Yes. Not a law which is often enforced but she had never told anyone about her other life and Sean could have wrecked everything for her just by showing up.'

'Blackmail?' Jo croaked.

'Sean was the kind of person who could never have enough money. He kept on asking Kelly and she kept on paying him off.' Macy paused and poured some more water for Jo. 'I'm hypothesising, of course.'

Jo wished she was in full voice and could remind him that he was always criticising her hypotheses. Instead she took a long drink and concentrated her energies on what she knew of Sean and Kelly. 'He was a pig to her when they were married. Connor told me that,' she said. Since she had learned that Sean and Kelly were married, she had been mentally comparing their charts and coming up with a clearer picture of them both. Kelly had mentioned during their consultation that both her parents had died when she was eleven and she had been brought up in a foster family. She must have married Sean when she was very young and been dependent on him. It would be in character for Sean to abuse this power. But when the worm finally turned, Kelly's isolation would make it easier for her to drop out of one life and start another.

It was beyond Jo to put this into words just then but Macy, whose mind was obviously running along the same lines, was saying, 'She must have made a new identity for herself when she walked out on him — but he caught up with her again somehow.'

'On the telly,' Jo said. 'She made an appeal when her little girl went missing.'

She saw Macy raise his dark eyebrows. 'Possibly. Anyway, Nick must also have known about her. Sean may even have told him,' he reflected.

'It figures — Cass said Sean was always boasting about—' Jo stopped to swallow with difficulty.

'His various scams?' Macy supplied. 'Yes, I can imagine that. He must have thought he could trust Nick as they were both in the shit together at work. But Sean underestimated how badly Nick wanted out of that mess. Nick didn't want his job going down the pan, whereas I don't think Sean cared.'

'Kelly was the ideal ally for Nick. They both wanted to get rid of Sean.' Jo took another gulp of water. 'Somehow he traced her and they arranged to kill Sean between them. I knew he must have had an accomplice.' She sank back on the pillow in satisfaction.

Macy stretched out his arms and studied the ceiling. 'It wouldn't have been that difficult to find Kelly,' he mused. 'Nick only had to follow Sean on one of his trips to the Midlands. Then he must have talked her into helping him get rid of her ex.'

'Maybe Kelly didn't need a lot of persuasion.'

Macy made an agreeing noise. 'She bought the car well in advance and went to meet Sean in it a few times so he got used to seeing her in it, chose the location — near the sailing club, which she belongs to — and set Sean up with a call saying her car had broken down. She was at the club then, highly visible behind the reception desk. I bet she even suggested to Nick what clothes to wear so he would look like her from the back. You know people see what they expect to see most of the time. And it was dusk. Sean was expecting to see Kelly and was used to the car. And that distinctive red-and-white jacket, that was hers, and it proved to be a pain.'

'Why on earth didn't Nick throw it away?'

'God knows. Kelly said they had agreed not to see each other again but Nick didn't stick to that. He kept ringing her up and asking to see her. It was like he got off on the idea of their being conspirators. She said she had to see him because Mark was making a fuss about the jacket. But I don't know,' Macy's handsome face wrinkled with doubt. 'More likely that was just an excuse to meet Nick one last time. I think she already decided he was too unreliable and she would be better off with him out of the way.'

'So she drugged him with something and drowned him in the pool.' Jo shuddered and her head pounded with the little movement. 'And tried to repeat the episode with me.'

'The difference was Nick was pretty drunk, according to the police,' Macy said, 'so he probably didn't put up much of a fight. It wasn't a bad plan. Merson — you know, the police inspector — told me it's very difficult to tell if someone has died by drowning. And if he's fully clothed and bone dry, it's not something they'd be looking for. She was going to dump him in the reservoir, I suppose, but those kids put her off. She put her bike in the back of Nick's car and just left him and cycled home.'

'We passed her,' Jo murmured. She was feeling battered but surprisingly better now that she had engaged her brain again. 'Sean made the classic mistake that Taureans can make — he let money rule his life. And he miscalculated about Nick. Never underestimate a Scorpio.'

'I'll remember that,' Macy said with an eye-roll, clearly unable to maintain his bedside manner for long. 'The stars didn't lead you to Kelly, did they? You thought Rosie was Nick's accomplice.'

'If I'd had an inkling there was a connection between Sean and Kelly, I'd have been looking for the right things in her chart.'

'You've always got a good excuse,' Macy countered. 'Anyway, you're very talkative for someone who's been half-strangled. What have you got to be so cheerful about?'

'I just remembered. I know where Connor is, so I can bill him for Sean's chart. And Kelly wrote me a cheque before I left the house.'

'She probably felt safe you wouldn't be around to cash it,' Macy grinned.

'True.' Jo gave a painful laugh. 'I was hoping she would recommend me to other people but I don't think she'll be moving in the same social circles now.'

'Maybe she'll tell Inspector Merson about you?'

'No good,' Jo croaked, 'he's a sceptical Capricorn. But I'll still get my best month's earnings for a while. And there's money coming from you—'

'All right,' Macy interrupted. 'You know I'll pay you. What were you saying about Taureans taking money too seriously?'

'I don't have to worry. I'm a Virgo. Just looking after the important details as usual.' Jo relaxed back on her pillow and smiled at him.

Her head still ached, and when she swallowed it felt as though someone was leaning on her neck, but despite this discomfort a feeling of satisfaction settled over her. She had told Connor she would find out what had happened to Sean and now she had.

THE END

ALSO BY LINDA MATHER

THE ZODIAC MYSTERIES
Book 1: FORECAST MURDER
Book 2: A SIGN FOR MURDER

Thank you for reading this book.

If you enjoyed it please leave feedback on Amazon or Goodreads, and if there is anything we missed or you have a question about, then please get in touch. We appreciate you choosing our book.

Founded in 2014 in Shoreditch, London, we at Joffe Books pride ourselves on our history of innovative publishing. We were thrilled to be shortlisted for Independent Publisher of the Year at the British Book Awards.

www.joffebooks.com

We're very grateful to eagle-eyed readers who take the time to contact us. Please send any errors you find to corrections@joffebooks.com. We'll get them fixed ASAP.